Across the Prairies
A Collection of Field Trial Articles, Interviews, and Original Stories

By Robert Franks

Across the Prairies: A Collection of Field Trial Articles, Interviews, and Original Stories

Cover photo copyright of Robert Franks
Cover design by Anthony Agreste
Book design by Virginia Agreste

ISBN: 978-0-578-31801-1

Printed by Lulu

1st Edition

All articles and stories, except The Wolves of Crow Mountain, are reprinted courtesy of *The American Field*

Dedicated to my wife Lisa, daughter Jessica, and granddaughters Rylie Jo and Allyn.

Table of Contents

✥ ARTICLES & INTERVIEWS ✥

Down a Dusty County Road—*Hoyle Eaton, Freddy Epp and Marshall Loftin*

Across the Prairies—*Andy Daugherty, John Rex Gates, Garland Priddy, and Billy Morton*

The Era of the Scout

The Southwestern, 1958–1977; The Best of Times

Four Great Dogs of John Rex Gates

Three of the Best—*Gordon Hazelwood, Shawn Kinkelaar, Harold Ray*

A Moment With One of the Best—*Harold Ray*

Tommy Olive Remembers

One In Ten Thousand

Down a Dusty Country Road

An interview with Hoyle Eaton, Freddie Epp, and Marshall Loftin

It is like taking a pickup down a dusty country road in the summer: slow, with the window rolled down and your elbow hanging out the side as you try to catch a breeze. The road is like many others in the South—lazy with views of pasture and field, giant oaks and pine, with neat white houses and abandoned homesteads. Around a bend in the road, I spot a couple of pointers stretched out in cool, green grass, dreaming of winter days and brown fence rows loaded with quail. Looking closely, I see three gentlemen sitting on the porch: Hoyle Eaton, Freddie Epp, and Marshall Loftin, enjoying cold Coca-Colas and the shade the porch provides against the scorching summer sun. I turn into the gravel drive as if directed by an unknown voice saying, "Welcome, sit a while." My experience interviewing each of these fine men reminded me of the above. Relaxed, truthful, humorous . . . sometimes direct to the point and with a true comfort and flavor that only comes through generations of family living in the South. Although conducted by phone, this visit had all the trappings of yesterday's stories told from a front porch swing like today's news. Each Hall of Famer exhibited a wealth of knowledge regarding bird dogs, field trialing, and life in general. Riggins White Knight, Red Water Rex, Blackbelt, Karate, and Monte Bello Peggy came to life once again and stretched out over the grass-covered prairie like derbys taking their first look at bird dog heaven. Stories are told, advice given, championships won, and old friends are remembered. Pull up a chair, sit, and pour a cold Coke while we visit with these three Hall of Famers.

When asked about his favorite field trialing memory, Hoyle Eaton knew just what story to tell. "It was when White Knight was a derby and had eighteen finds at the National Championship. For the first half of the brace, it was cloudy and drizzling rain. The birds were running and not setting. When encountering scent, he would walk with his head and tail up; he was not trying to take the birds out or stalking the birds but was trying to make body contact with them. I think that is what the judges mostly criticized him for, but for the last hour and a half there was not even a slight bobble. He had three coveys in the last ten minutes. It was an ideal bird day and not real cold. This was just opposite to the day when White Knight won the National. It was fourteen degrees when they turned him loose, with snow and ice all over everything. He tore his feet up and the ice sliced his legs open. He inhaled so much of that cold air that it frostbit his lungs, and he developed a cough that stayed with him for the rest of his life."

When asked if he thought White Knight had a chance of winning the National as a derby with eighteen finds, Eaton replied, "Well, yeah! I had some old-time judges who knew dogs tell me if they would have been judging, he would have won it. He did a great job that day, and it would have been hard for any dog to go through three hours and eighteen finds without a bobble."

Freddie Epp seemed to be waiting for this question. "I bought a young derby, The Hub, from Cary Clary. The dog was in Georgia at the time, and I sent my son to pick him up. He was a nice dog, and I took him to Canada that summer. He was making progress but cut his leg on something. Because of the cut, I wasn't able to work him as much as I would have liked. When we got him home, I finished breaking him and started to get him in condition. I was going to the Florida Championship Derby, and I thought . . . well, I'll just run him myself, and pay the entry fee, and give him some experience. When we got there, here came T.J. Robertson and Hal Brooks with a young doctor. He was hoping to get into the field trial game and wanted to know if I had any dogs for sale. I passed it off as I didn't think they were serious, and I started putting the horses up and feeding my dogs. Later that afternoon this doctor walks up, sort of bashful, and wanted to know where was the dog I had for sale. I pointed to the derby I had who was late in getting broke. I told him that he was a little behind the other dogs and was really not capable of winning this trial; I just brought him for the experience. He wanted to know what I wanted for him, and I said $1,500.00. I passed it off and didn't think much more about it until we were in the club house drawing the trial and I saw the doctor sitting there. I had entered the dog in the derby; there were about forty dogs entered. I hollered at him and said, 'Hey, Doc, I entered the dog in your name where you could have a dog running here.' Well, we ran the derby and I won the forty-four dog derby with this little dog. When they announced the winners, the young doctor, Dr. Littell, heard that and he said, 'That's my dog.' He is now my son-in-law! Bob Crenshaw was one of the judges, and he said, 'How lucky can a man be! I've been running dogs all my life, and I don't ever think I had a win this good. Here he just gets a dog and wins.'"

Pausing just a minute to think, Marshall Loftin began. "I was running Kreole at the National Free-for-All, which had three-hour heats. I had sent Kreole to the front just before the course made a big turn to the right. He missed the turn, and I lost track of him. The course made several other turns, and we ended up in a big field. When it got close to pick up time, I didn't see him, but I decided to walk out where the judges couldn't see and point him out to the front even thought I had no idea where he actually was. At the Free-for-All, you did not have to put a rope on the dog after three hours and pick your dog up. I blew my scout in like I knew where the dog was. As he was riding in, I pointed the dog out again. The three owners of Kreole were in the gallery and started talking among themselves asking if any of them could see the dog. They couldn't, but one finally said, 'Don't worry, Marshall's looking at him.' At that time the judges ordered him up, and I took off in a hard run right where I pointed him out, and sure enough, he came out of the sage grass right where I had been pointing. When that son-of-a-gun came up to me that day, I was some proud! Kreole won the Free-for-All that day."

When asked about his favorite story while training on the prairie, Freddie Epp replied, "Our dog camp had been set up in a new area. We were new to the country around this camp although the locals had shown me around a little bit. RuthAnn was driving the dog truck, and we were starting to work the dogs. We would look at the horizon and find a tree or something and tell RuthAnn to drive the truck there any way she could. Our party would take the dogs and run, meet her, and turn some more out. The ranchers had told us that there was a wire fence, which went straight west for about two miles, so we headed west. I figured it kept on going, but what we didn't know is that the fence ran out after a way. The dogs were tired and wore out after we rode about five miles north looking for a fence. It was me, my scout, and my two boys. At this time we picked up the dogs. When we did not get back to the truck, RuthAnn finally gave up and went back to the camp. About four in the evening, we hit a line fence going east and west, so we followed it for about three miles and then hit another one going south, which we hoped would bring us back toward camp. Going through a thicket of trees, we jumped some deer which got the dogs all excited. We managed to hold on to the dogs and later came on another fence, which we figured was north of camp. After spending all day lost, we finally got back to camp about six-thirty that evening."

"It was when Cherokee Jake attacked my horse!" Mr. Eaton had no doubt which story he was going to tell. "The first time Cherokee Jake was turned out on the prairie was also the first time he had been around a horse. He must have thought that the horse was some sort of a bad monster who was going to hurt me, as he was hitting him in the back legs and thighs and was making the blood fly. It took me a while to get the horse calmed down as it went to kicking and bucking. I finally got off him and was lucky not to get hurt. When everything calmed down I had one of the helpers walk beside the horse with the dog, and I could see that he realized that the horses were just a part of the program. I turned him loose, and he went to attacking cattle just like he was attacking the horse. We caught him again, and I had a helper lead him through the cattle for about thirty minutes. He never had a problem with a cow or horse again. After this we turned him loose on the prairie, and he went straight to the front. He disappeared over a rise in the prairie. When we caught up with him, he was locked up on point, and I flushed two chickens in front of him. He was broke steady to wing and shot after that."

Marshall Loftin remembered like yesterday the greatest performance he had ever seen. "It was at the 1957 National Free-for-All in Canton, Mississippi. It featured two great handlers, two great scouts, and two great dogs. Clyde Morton and his scout Man Rand were running Palamonium, and John Gates and his scout Peck Kelly were running Medallion. The gallery was there and during the trial they would say, 'I think Clyde is beating him,' but thirty minutes later, 'I think John is winning.' It just went back and forth, back and forth. Medallion won it and in 1958 the same pair were braced. Medallion won it even though the brace was not nearly as good as the year before. I think one of 'em had six finds and the other one seven. The gallery was kind of split; half of 'em were for Clyde Morton, and the other half were for John Gates."

Mr. Loftin further recalled another great performance. "I judged the Illinois Shooting Dog Championship in 1979. I wanted to place Little Diamond, and the other judge wanted to place Great Notion.

This being the case, we called them back for a second series. We decided to run the dogs thirty minutes and then talk. I told the boys that one of these dogs will be the champion, the other would be the runner-up, and all the other dogs could go home. We ran the dogs for two hours and five minutes before they untied themselves. Toward the end, Little Diamond started to get tired with Great Notion being stronger. Larry Moon handled Great Notion and Fred Rayl Little Diamond. I have heard some of the shooting dog men say that that was the greatest performance ever in a shooting dog trial."

Freddie Epp related a performance by an amateur dog his daughter RuthAnn ran in south Alabama. "It was in the Charlie Farquhar Memorial stake that my daughter ran her dog, Just Denver. He was sometimes a run-off kind of dog but still a lot of dog. Bill Mason was scouting for her, and she had talked me into going and watching them. It started raining and that ole dog ran all over the world. He was running so hard that a member of the gallery shouted to please put a rope on the dog as he was running so hard, he was bound to get away. Bill rode all over the country and found him on point five times. It was some performance! I know there have been a lot of great open performances, but I thought that was one of the best I ever saw. There was no doubt about it; he was just a tough ole dog. One time he was lost running in an amateur trial at Mortlatch, and some guys found him over twenty miles away. He was to run the next day at the region fourteen championship and had knocked all the pads off his feet. RuthAnn fed him up, turned him loose, and he won the championship. He was a real chicken dog. No counterfeit dogs make it on the prairies, and he sure was not a counterfeit dog."

"When White Knight won the Free-for-All in 1967, it was the greatest performance I have ever witnessed," Hoyle Eaton said with pride. "It had rained the day before and all night. Water was standing everywhere. About seven that morning when it quit raining, the temperature went to dropping. By the time we turned him loose at eight, it was freezing. On his first find, we found him pointed to the front. He was sitting down and I thought, boy, what are you doing? I just couldn't understand it. But when I got close to him, I could see that his tail was just a big icicle, and water had frozen to him on the underside. Even though he was sitting down, he had the birds. I showed the ice to the judges, and they did not hold it against him. When I turned him loose after flushing birds, it warmed up just enough to get the ice off him. It was so wet that every time his feet would hit the ground, water would splash up on him. With about twenty minutes to go in the brace, he was nearing the sand road close to the clubhouse. There was a creek on the left that wasn't normally real wide, but with all the rain, it was flowing at the top of the bank with really swift water. I tried to get him to come with me and cross the bridge with the horses, but when he saw a ditch, he would always look to see which way I was going, and he would jump it and go with me. He got to the creek and thought he could jump it. He jumped, and his front feet hit the bank on the other side, but his back end hit the water. The swift current pulled him into the creek, and he drifted down the creek in the cold water until he got to the bridge and was able to get out of the creek. I thought he was done and knew he would not be able to finish. I got to him with a towel that I had on my saddle, dried him off the best I could, and sent him on. There were many deep horse tracks around this area because of the mud, and he would hit the horse tracks and just stagger. When he finally got out of the tracks, he went on top of a hill, and that's where I saw him straight ahead on point. I said, well, he may finish. I went to him, flushed the birds, and sent him on as there were just a few minutes left. White Knight went out of sight in a wood line, and Joe Hurdle, one of the judges, wanted to ride ahead with me and see how he would finish. When we caught sight of him, he was hunting like the dickens, running that wood line. Shortly after, he finished the brace and won the trial. It was the most gutsy performance I have ever seen other than possibly Ormand Smart Alec when he won the Free-for-All."

When asked when he first thought White Knight might be something special, Mr. Eaton quickly replied, "I had worked White Knight's sister, Stanley's Candy. At that point in my career, I did not have the experience I needed to really evaluate a dog, but an old friend Dick Brown did. We decided he might be something special one day when I had White Knight and a littermate running in a pasture down at my dad's farm. He was around four months old and took off out in the pasture like a streak of lightning, chasing every kind of bird he could find. You could see he was putting every ounce of effort he could into it. Dick told me right off the bat that there might be something special in the dog. I worked him almost every day and did not let him lay in the kennel. I knew at that time that he was something special; I just didn't know how special he would be."

Freddie Epp shared this story when asked about the most intelligent dog he had ever seen. "I had an ole setter meat dog that was a great bird dog. One day my cousin and I were hunting and had gotten into some single birds. We had the setter and an ole pointer down at the time. I looked around and could not find the setter, and I knew that about a quarter a mile over the hill there was another covey. I figured he had probably gone on to them, and I told my cousin that the other dog was pointed, and I was going to walk up on the hill and see what was going on. Sure enough when I got to the top of the hill, there he was pointed. I went and got my cousin, and we headed up there and found that the dog was gone. Just before we got to the fence corner where I had seen him pointed, he came running, jumped a fence, and came right up there where he was pointed, and points again. We kicked and there was sure enough a covey of birds right where he said. We shot those birds, we sent him on, and he went the way he had come back. It wasn't long before he had a covey pointed, and you can suppose a lot of things, but I know he wanted to find birds so badly while we were wasting time shooting singles that he went and pointed that second covey beyond the rise. When we were slow getting there, he backed off the covey and found another covey to know where they were. When we got up there, he points 'em both again."

"The smartest field trail dog I ever had was Karate," continued Epp. "He always knew where the front was. We were at the United States Chicken Championship one year, and they had put water troughs around the course. On the last day of the trial, the state folks came and took all the water troughs up where they would not have to come back. I was roading Karate near the spot where a water trough had been the day before, and ole karate was pulling towards the spot because he remembered and wanted a drink of water."

"Without a doubt it was Red Water Rex," Hoyle Eaton said without having to pause to think. "When I would attempt a flush, and he wasn't getting any body scent from the birds, Rex would start whimpering and barking real short and choppy. He was fussing at me, wanting me to turn him loose to show me where the birds had run to. I would go back and release him with everybody, saying he was going to knock the birds. He never would. He would throw his head in the air and go to weaving and cat walking until he would get the body scent again and then he would point."

"Monte Bello Peggy," was Marshall Loftin's reply. "If she did something wrong and you corrected her, she would never make the same mistake twice. She was the best field trial dog I have seen in my lifetime. Peggy won the Amateur Championship with her owner, beating Ferrell Miller. She was second in the Purina Top Dog of the Year for three years in a row."

With a laugh, Hoyle Eaton recounted his two favorite dog stories. "It was what I called White Knight's last fling. We would take him to the prairie with us in the summertime just to let him play, to have a big time, and to get him out of the Mississippi heat. He was fourteen, and he stayed in the house. We would always let him outside at noon when we would come in from working dogs. He would go out into the yard, dig for ground gophers, and play. This particular day it had rained, and several trainers were at my camp sitting in the yard talking. White Knight was playing in the black dirt. When he was through, he brushed against me telling me he wanted back into the house. When I looked at him, I started fussing at him real strong because he had that ole black dirt all over his face and his chest. I told him, 'Bud, get yourself down to the pond, clean yourself up and then I might let you back into the house.' I was saying that for the benefit of the other trainers that were around. I had no idea that he would, but he went straight to that pond and stayed down there a little bit. When he came back, he had it all cleaned off except two little streaks under an eye. I looked at him and said, 'That's a pretty good job, and I'll let you into the house now.' Another thing he did was when we went to Paducah to the field trials, I would stay at the Holiday Inn. I let him out of the truck to piddle around while I took my stuff to the room. This particular time, I got my bags and called and called for him to go to the room, but he didn't respond. I called again, and he still didn't respond. I was beginning to get a little worried as there were streets around there and with the traffic, I got pretty nervous. I called and called, and he still didn't come. I thought a minute, and I figured out what he did. He remembered where we stayed the year before, and he had already gone to the room. That was upstairs on the backside of the motel. Sure enough I went to that room, and there he sat waiting on me."

"It was when Roy won the Continental Derby Championship with Morning Edition," Mr. Epp replied with pride. "We called him Beef; ole Beef was a lot of dog. If you didn't work him a lot, you couldn't keep up with him. We were staying with Mr. Charles Osmond at Merryway Plantation, which is about twenty-five miles from the Dixie where they run the Continental. He was to run the second brace in the afternoon. Roy and I worked him two hours that morning at the Merryway Plantation so we could wear him down. When it came time for the second brace, we turned him loose. Roy was running him and I was scouting for him. Beef didn't start too strong, and Roy said, 'Daddy, I believe we worked him too long.' But it didn't take him long to warm up, and he was running like the wind. On his first find, Beef was pointing the birds in

Florida, and we flushed them in Georgia. (Note the Dixie plantation grounds encompass both Florida and Georgia.) He then had another find. And he was running big, big, big, then we lost him. Roy was going on to the front, and I tracked Beef into a swamp and then sort of lost him. I came up to the water in the swamp and I thought, he is gone, and I will just water my horse and turn around where I could cut around to the front. 'Bout that time I heard something panting, and I looked up and here came old Beef. I threw him in heel, caught up with Roy, and sent Beef right out to the front. About to lose him again, I ran into the Rayl's scout, Joe Bush, and he said, 'He went right in that ole graveyard.' I finally caught up with him and sent him back up to the front. He was running really big, and I couldn't see him half the time. Roy Gimes was riding front for us, and he could see him every now and then and would point him out. When the judges hollered pick up time, we ended up right in a big ole swamp. So Beef had two finds, had run all over the world, and was gone at pick up. Roy went on forward, the judges stopped, and they were waiting to see him pick Beef up. I sort of covered the country around to the side and rode back up to the judges. They wanted to know if Roy had him. I looked way off into the swamp, and I saw Roy on his horse heading toward us. The judges asked me if Roy had him. I said I don't know, but I see a rope running out in front of that horse, and there has got to be something pulling it! As Roy come out from some trees, the judge, George Evans from Texas, was loving the dog, and he said, 'I don't need to see any more.' And they jumped in the car and off they went. Ole Beef's race that day was sort of the excitement that keeps you going with 'em."

"Leon Covington," Mr. Loftin said. "The funniest things that happened in my field trial career were surrounded by Leon Covington."

When asked who he thought was the greatest stud dog of his generation, Marshall Loftin recalled many of the greatest dogs and handlers of all time. "There were so many great sires that I don't think there was just one. You can go way back yonder to Stilla's

Wahoo Pete—that was John Gates's dog. He produced Medallion, who won the Free-for-All twice. Susan Peters was a littermate to them, and she was inducted into the Hall of Fame. Hoyle had White Knight, and he was a really great stud dog. Gunsmoke . . . I remember ole Gunsmoke really well. Look at the winning dogs he produced. He didn't produce as many winnin' all-age dogs as shooting dogs. Another one was the Wrangler dog from Texas who produced The Arkansas Ranger, who won the National, and Hattie of Arkansas. I also liked Paladin's Royal Flush. His daddy, Paladin's Royal Air, produced a lot of good dogs. One of the nicest dogs you ever saw was A Rambling Rebel. You see most trainers had their own breeding program. Fred Arant had the Rambling Rebel dogs, John Gates had Satilla Wahoo Pete, Howard Kirk had Gunsmoke, Hoyle Eaton had White Knight, and he won the National with Miller's White Cloud."

Hoyle Eaton replied emphatically, "White Knight. It's been over forty years and his linage is still winning today. That's the mark of a great sire."

Freddie Epp agreed. "It would have to be Riggins White Knight. He sired Miller's Chief and the other white dogs that came down through Ferrell Miller. All those dogs go back to Riggins White Knight."

Training secrets are what all trainers cherish, sometimes guard, and on occasion share. Freddie Epp had this to say regarding his best training secret: "Hard work! Get up and put those dogs on the ground. They can't learn nothing in the kennel. I always liked to look at a dog's eyes. I know you have to punish them some to get them broke but, always watch your dog's eyes. No matter what the praise or punishment, always look at his eyes, and he will tell you what you should do. If he gets too glassy-eyed, you had better quit and come back later."

Hoyle Eaton was short and to the point. "Give the dog the time and experience to develop his own natural abilities."

A reply in a manner that is Marshall Loftin at his best: "That's a secret I don't tell!"

When asked about mistakes today's trainers make, Mr. Eaton commented, "They want instant perfection by means of the electric collar and liberated birds."

Mr. Loftin said, "Dog trainers today in many cases are handlers and not trainers. They buy their dogs already trained. Back when we all came along, we had to take our dog and train 'em and run 'em as a derby, then wait for them to come to All Age."

Freddie Epp offered some very sound advice. "Today's handlers win a lot and make a good living, but quite a few of them have a lot of dogs. They all have four wheelers and work the dogs on the four wheelers because time is short and they have to get all of them roaded. A dog doesn't learn much being roaded by a four wheeler. About all they learn is to run roads. When I was running, we would road all our dogs on horseback. You could take them around a bush, you could talk to them, and you could put them on a bird. You could make them whoa, and they could learn something all the time you were roading them. Now you see a lot of dogs just go right down the course where the horses go and they don't think at all."

"Training methods have changed over the last forty years," Freddy Epp relayed. "The electronics have made a big difference. Forty years ago when I was running, you had to outsmart dogs, you had to run 'em down, tag 'em back, or catch 'em. If we had one who was a trailer, we would get rid of 'em. Nowadays they just give a trailer the juice and some make good dogs. The problem here is that they breed these dogs and they produce more trailers. There is nothing better than hands-on training. This reminds me of a story of how we broke Blackbelt. We were near a little patch of bushes where we generally find a covey of birds. We had Blackbelt pointing birds pretty well, but when we would get there, he would want to jump in 'em. This was before electric collars. I put a rope on him and let him pull it. I sent my son Ed around on the other side where we always find birds and had him get in there and lay down in the grass about where I figured Blackbelt would come in and point. I kinda guided him, and shore enough, he went in there and pointed that covey of birds. Ed was close enough that he just crawled up and grabbed the end of that rope. I rode up to him slowly and as soon as I did, he busted in there on the birds, and Ed jumped up and snatched him down with that rope. It surprised him so that he was broke from that day on. That's the difference from today to yesterday. You had to figure little things to do to outsmart the dog."

Marshall Loftin agreed with Mr. Epp. "Electric collars and the GPS are great things. When you are working dogs, they can pick up bad habits very quickly. While a dog is out there running around by himself, he is picking up bad habits. With the GPS you can just go get him. A lot of dogs pick up their bad habits when they point, and you can't find them. They stand there, stand there, and stand there until they bust 'em and then go and play with the singles. You don't have this with the GPS. All this modern stuff makes training dogs a lot easier."

"Lack of training grounds and wild birds," was Hoyle Eaton's reply. "Years ago when training on wild birds, it was the dog's responsibility to go find them. Today it is required that the dog stay between ten and two in front of the horse because that's where the liberated birds have been planted. To me this restricts a dog's bird-finding ability. I was never thrilled by a mechanical dog's performance."

Some great names came up when these three Hall of Famers were asked about their mentors. Marshall Loftin replied, "Bill Cosner taught me to not get in too much of a hurry when training a dog. I applied this principle to my training. Each month I would think about the dogs that I was training and evaluate them. I would always ask myself if they were making any progress. If the dog was making progress, even a little, I would keep him. I never tried to push a dog's training too hard or fast. The first time he was worse than he was a month ago, we quit him."

Hoyle Eaton credits much of his knowledge of dogs to his life growing up on a farm. "My mentor was my upbringing around the barn, being around animals all my life. When I first started, I had a couple of unregistered pointer pups, and I got acquainted with Hall of Famer Dick Brown. He had a little female called Candy N Cake. He took the American Field, I got to reading it and then subscribed to it. After reading the Field for some time and being around Mr. Brown, I asked him to inquire if Martin Davis, who owned a half interest in Stanley's Candy, the mother of White Knight, if he would sell me his half of her. Mr. Brown did, and he agreed to sell her to me for thirty-five dollars. I asked him if I could pay him five dollars down and five dollars a week until I had her paid for. He agreed, and we bred her back to Major Lexington's Boy. That was the breeding that produced White Knight. Dick knew dogs and knew what an all-age dog should look like on the ground and around birds. I learned that the secret to training dogs is to get them to know what you are trying to teach them and to communicate with them well enough to get the point across without taking anything out of the dog.

Freddie Epp had two of the best. "I had Clyde Morton and John Gates. I was so thankful. I thought I had the two greatest trainers that ever trained. Mr. Clyde never did tell you a whole lot. He made you go with him and taught you by doing. He always told me that you have got to make those dogs handle, but don't teach them too good or those other trainers will take them away from you. Man Rand, who was his scout, also taught me a great deal. Man taught me that when you want to punish a dog, pick him up and bite his ear. That was a pretty good little trick as the dog did not like his ear getting bit. John Gates taught me when to quit. When you get a dog that has learned something, don't just keep pouring it to him, put him up and let him absorb it. In Canada, dogs would get tired of chickens. Evidently they do not smell as good as quail, and if you work 'em a lot and don't kill 'em any, they get tired of them. So, when you get to a point with the dogs, you have to recognize it and pick 'em up. John Gates was the greatest at reading a dog, knowing when they had learned a lesson, and to know when to put them up. Both these men were hard workers; they taught me to get up and work hard."

Good scouts are incredibly hard to find and are invaluable. When asked who the greatest scouts were, some names of the past came alive. Freddie Epp commented that his son Roy was as good as ever rode. He thought for a moment and said, "Man Rand, who scouted for Clyde and Billy Morton, gets my vote. He had a way of looking like he was doing nothing but he was really getting the dogs to the front. He was very quiet and didn't show off, putting the focus on the dog."

"That can't be answered," came Mr. Loftin's strong reply. "Now I know your next question is going to be why. I had a scout, L.S. Dunn, who was a real fine scout for me. Peck Kelly, John Gates's scout, was probably the best all around. Man Rand was an excellent scout for Clyde Morton. Robert was an outstanding scout for Hoyle Eaton. My son, Billy Loftin, was an awfully good scout; he scouted for Monte Bello Peggy. It's a scout and handler combination. It's just like two boys playing basketball: they have got to know each other. You know that scouts not only help scout but they help you train the dogs. Most of them have a string of young dogs to work on the prairies just like the trainers. The scouts have to know how the trainer does things. Man Rand went into the Hall of Fame, and I think Peck Kelly should be in the Hall of Fame as he was a top-notch scout. All of these scouts are good when paired with the handlers they work for. If they were paired with another handler, they might not be a success. I never hired a scout that scouted for another man. I wanted things done my way."

Hoyle Eaton stated, "Man Rand, Peck Kelly, who scouted for John Gates, were very good and then Robert, the man who scouted for me, was hard to beat."

The hot afternoon sun is giving way to the long shadows that signal twilight and the relief it brings from the heat of the day. Locusts sing, people venture out to enjoy the cool of the evening, and mosquitoes begin to look for a late afternoon meal. It's time to leave, goodbyes are said, and I head for my truck with distinct memories of these gentlemen and their recollections. Before I reach my truck, I turn, and Marshall Loftin leaves this last bit of wisdom with me to ponder: "My life has been in the best of the field trial game that there will ever be. I believe this. I got to run at the National when you could point fifteen or eighteen coveys of wild birds in the three hours. In the Continental, I pointed twelve coveys of wild birds with Monte Bello Peggy. Now they are releasing birds at the National. It was a privilege to be running in the best time of field trialing." With that thought still in my head, I point my truck toward home. The dust from the gravel road partially obscures the white house as I look back in the rearview mirror of my pickup. I say to myself, "Today was one of my best days."

1987 National Free-for-All Champion Kreole is posed with handler Marshall Loftin joined by Ben "Man" Rand and scout Darren Hudson

Photo courtesy of The American Field

Freddie Epp poses 1980 United States Open winner Yoshi Blackbelt Fargo. Standing from left: Verle Farrow, Ed Mack Farrior, and Jimmy Hinton
Photo courtesy of The American Field

Hoyle Eaton and Red Water Rex
Photo courtesy of The American Field

Freddy Epp with Purina Award winner Blackbelt
Photo courtesy of RuthAnn Epp

Across the Prairies

I wonder if, while watching their dads handle dogs on the open, endless prairie, John Rex Gates and Andy Daugherty realized they were watching the best God had placed on this earth? Would youngsters Garland Priddy and Billy Morton, bird hunting with their dads on cold, bleak afternoons, envision their handprint being placed upon some of the finest trial dogs to ever live and be considered among the elite of history's trainers? Did these men learn the ethic of hard work and honesty from their proud parents? I think so. It was with pride that I intervened these four gentlemen whose lives, exploits, and dogs will live forever in field trial lore.

The wide, northern prairies are a magical place for dogs and handlers alike. There is no place better in the world to mold bird dogs than the prairie. It is the perfect place to create lifetime memories. Andy Daugherty, who met his wife there, shared that he has been going to the prairies for forty-eight years and that working dogs is the most fun you have up there.

"I would quit training if I couldn't go to the prairie. There is nothing quite as beautiful as watching a prairie dog run, work the wind, and come in downwind from the birds. It takes a lot of birds to make a tremendous prairie dog, and in the sixties and seventies we had lots and lots of birds. It's fun working dogs up there because it is cool and you can work dogs all day. I loved going with my dad and have great memories of those times. He had us work and ride hard, but it was still fun. When I was young, it was different than it is now; at that time I thought summer would never end. Now, when I get there, time seems to go in a flash; you just get there and the next thing you know you are running in trials. I learned watching the best. Bill Rayl had great prairie dogs along with Stub Poynor. I rode and watched Joe Odem, Tommy Long, and Robert Burris and how they got dogs to come around. I loved to watch the great ones. There was nothing like watching Fred Arant's dogs run the prairies and the truly outstanding dogs John Rex had. The first year I went to trials up there was 1970, and I don't think I have missed any since."

John Rex Gates remembered that Andy was notorious in his younger years on the prairie for riding by you and snatching your bridle, slapping the horse on the hindquarters, and hollering, "Get it, cowboy!" Many a rider was sent across the prairie with a horse bucking and carrying on.

"My first trip to the prairie was when Wrap Up was a derby," Billy Morton was quick to reply. "I thought it was the greatest place in the world when we got there. We didn't have all of the conveniences; we had to haul our water in and had a gas stove to cook on. That didn't make any difference. It was just seeing that big ole open country with those bluffs and hedge rows, learning about chickens, and check cording dogs through there. The time you can work dogs on the prairie is amazing. You can get in ten to twelve hours a day easy and somewhere in there you kinda get a little nap, if you can, in the middle of the day.

"I still remember everything Hoyle Eaton taught me up there that first summer. Tommy Olive was also up there. He was a good dog trainer and was working and scouting for Hoyle. I think he was scouting for Rex when he won the national. I had Wrap Up and I didn't know what you could do with dogs on the prairie. When they would come in and take a little nap in the middle of the day, I'd go out there and get a check cord and I'd take my dogs back down to the bluffs where some young chickens were that I didn't tell anyone about. Cov's trial was one of the first trials up there. I turned my dog loose, and she ran out there about a hundred yards and stopped, turned, and just looked back at me. Hoyle, Tommy, and Robert, and all of 'em like ta fell off their horse.

"Hoyle just couldn't quit laughing. He said, 'There was no use in me telling ya not to work that dog that much. If I would have tried to tell you that you would have thought I was going to try to beat you.' I put her up and we went to Cov's about a week later and that puppy ran the best race I'd seen in a long time. Hoyle said so too. I remember Leon Covington sitting over there on a hill in an ole Dodge truck, and when we got through, Cov said, 'Boy'—he always called me boy—'That's a good puppy there—don't break her too quick." We worked hard and everybody had the dogs divided up. Each one of us had about twenty dogs. You could work ten of them a day if you got out there and got with it."

A humorous story regarding Mr. Morton was told by Hoyle Eaton. "We were helping a local rancher get his calves up, brand and castrate them. When the banding was over, the Canada boys would always have a little rodeo. The Canadian boys got some calves in a pen and rode two or three of them or tried to. Then they started in, 'Why don't those Yanks get on one of these bulls?' Hoyle told them that they could try all they wanted but he wasn't about to get on one of them. Right after that, Billy decided that he would give it a try. That bull bucked once or twice and throwed him right up in the air, and he came down and landed on his head. He was knocked out cold! When he came to, I was standing over him laughing."

Garland Priddy started working dogs in the early 1970s in Alberta. "The days were long and you had the bluffs that you could teach your young dogs to go to—nearly all of them had chicken in them. It was big, open country with very few fences where your nearest neighbor was two or three miles away and the next one six or seven miles away. Marshall Loftin and I camped together there in the seventies and eighties and had almost unlimited grounds. It was great working with Marshall, by working together it was like we were always in field trial scenarios every day. Some days we would have fifteen or sixteen people riding with us, so many days it was like working in a field trail. It was very good for the dogs. Marshall remembered the days with Garland on the prairies fondly. "We camped together for twelve or thirteen years and never disagreed on nothing. He was fun to be around, a good man, and a very good handler." Field trial-wise, Mortlach in the seventies and eighties was just a tremendous place. It was wide open and they had birds nearly every year. There was never a course you could not win it on. You couldn't hide anything and you had to have a true all-age dog to compete. I've seen many great performances there."

"I remember one time at a field trial on the prairie," John Rex Gates recalled, "a boy called a point about a mile from where the dog was supposed to be. He jumped down off his horse, jumped in and flushed a sharp tail and hollered, "There they go, judge." The judge said, 'Where is your dog?' and the boy said, 'He is standing there right off the edge of this bush.' Well, there wasn't a dog there but a big ole rock. We rode a mile to see him flush a chicken from in front of a rock! The prairie teaches dogs how to hunt, especially into the wind. In Canada, we had what we called bluffs, which were small bushes scattered across the prairie. On up in the day from around ten in the morning up until four in the afternoon, the sharp-tail would bush up, which taught a dog to go and hunt where the birds are. It also teaches the dogs how to use the wind to go up to that bush. If they don't use the wind, they will run into that bush and flush the birds. Up there, it will teach a dog to go around the bush, use the wind, and smell the birds. This is a beautiful thing to see as they will learn to throw that head up and go into the wind. It is probably one of the greatest places in the world to go and work young dogs."

A funny story was told on Andy Daugherty by John Rex Gates that revolved around his dad and brother. "The Daughertys were running Dr. Hawthorne's dog at the National. The night before the running, Bud gave Andy a pretty good little talking-to. Andy's brother also happened to be down there. He and Andy had a habit of going out and prowling around at night a little bit. Bud said that afternoon, 'Boys, I'm gonna tell you one thing. We are going to eat supper tonight and then go to that motel room and all three of us are going to be in bed by eight o'clock. We got our best dog to run in the morning and ain't nobody going out tonight.' Andy and his uncle had gone into a little country store and got what they called itching power. They went back to the motel and put the itching power all in Bud's bed. Bud took him a big shower when they got home and crawled into bed and started itching like crazy. The itching power was just tearing him up. He jumped up out of bed and said, 'Boys, get up, I think there is bugs in my bed.' They looked and couldn't find any. Bud told them he was going to take another shower and go back to bed. While he was in the shower, they put some more of the itching power in his bed. Needless to say no one in that room was asleep by eight. Bud found about it the next day and it is a wonder Andy is still alive."

Upon asking these gentlemen about the greatest performance they had witnessed by a dog other than their own, this author was surprised how quickly and emphatically each replied. Garland Priddy remembered the day Crossmatch won the Continental. "When he ran, if it wasn't ninety degrees, it was close to it. He was turned loose about two-thirty p.m. in the worst of the heat that day. Jimmy Palmer, who was working with me, saw him pointing under an ole oak tree from a truck we were in. They would have never found him if not for Jimmy. I don't think there were many dogs down there that day that could have gone through the heat. He had either seven or nine finds and I thought it was an outstanding performance. Bud Daugherty was running him and he went on to win the National that year. He was sometimes a rough handling dog, but on that day he was not."

John Rex Gates remembered training Crossmatch for the Continental. "Crossmatch was a hell of a bird dog but was also a pretty good outlaw. Bud wanted to really work him down and get him into a lot of birds. We worked him almost a full day down in sand country in south Georgia and shot a bunch of birds over him, then rested him for a day, and the next day we worked him for another long term. To work him down, we put a roading harness with a good long rope and two logging chains on him. Bud had four of us watching that dog. We did not want him to get away. We basically brought him down and bird hunted him for two days. It was a thrill for all of us that he came through like he did. We all knew he had it in him."

"Silverwood, handled by Robin Gates in Florida." Andy Daugherty didn't think twice. "He had four finds in the Florida Championship and I thought he was unbeatable. After seeing him run, I started thinking to myself how I was going to beat him. I couldn't out-bird him. You can't outrun him. He handled perfect and you can't beat the way Robin handled him. When I got to the barn I said, 'There is no way to beat him.' It was just a perfect brace where you could ride and watch a super dog handled perfectly. He was immaculate on his game, hunted all the right places and stayed dead ahead of us. Robin Gates commented on the performance. It was kinda a Cinderella story with that dog. He was a hell of a dog. It was the best performance bar none I have ever seen. Me handling or someone else handling. I knew about twenty minutes after the break away that if something didn't happen this was going to be a special performance. He was a big dog, close to seventy pounds and when he pointed he looked like a bear out there. He was beautiful around his game. I had seen Silverwood run the fall before and he had had all sorts of health issues, Luke Weaver shared, and I thought the dog would never run again. I was judging the Florida Champion that year and they turned Silverwood loose on the second morning course which is the prettiest course down there. It is all rolling hills and you can see a dog forever. They turned the dog a ©loose and I think he had four finds. I think on his fourth find he and his bracemate were coming up a fire break next to a highway. They swapped heads and the bracemate went on to the front and Silverwood pointed a covey. It was a super find. At the end of the hour he was dead to the front and just a few minutes after pickup they had him, it was just a remarkable performance. When we went to lunch that day they were having a birthday party for Colvin Davis. He got up and said, "Boys, we are running for runner-up." And he still had dogs to run. That's how good a performance it was. They called him "Big" and he was big. I saw him win the Continental in the Piney woods down there and he looked like a picture. He was big, strong and high-tailed and a super athlete, I don't know of another dog that was in his class at that time.

The trial Billy Morton remembered the most was when Riggins White Knight didn't win the National as a derby. "I had been scouting for Hoyle and we had won the National Derby Championship. That qualified us for the National with ole Bud. We didn't know very much at the time regarding all the things we had to do to present Bud well at the National. Jack Harper helped Hoyle and myself more than anybody. Mr. Jack wasn't far from there and would come over there and run dogs with us. I've still got the letter he wrote me telling me what a scout should do. There are some little things in there that you wouldn't think about. He told us all they were trying to do up there (the National), and he was right. I never saw anything like Bud that day, he was flying. Everyone in the country had heard about him and wanted to see him run. We turned him loose on the breakaway. He faded out across the front and we didn't know where he was. We were braced with Paul Walker. Peck Kelly was scouting for John Gates and really helped me a lot that day. We rode and rode, and I looked at the country and I pretty much knew where he was going to head. I went down by a real thick thicket and he was standing in it with a covey of birds pointed to the front of him. All I could see sticking up was his tail. It looked like that day evera' thing just went right. I couldn't miss him every time I would go out.

"Sometimes Hoyle would get excited and wouldn't call his Scout back in, so I had to get somebody in the gallery that I could trust to call Scout in whenever the dog would show up. I think it was Dick Dumas that was one of the judges. After the first find we had gotten way behind. I jumped on my horse and heeled Bud, which he was real good at doing although he would jump up and bark at you. We started up and the judge said, 'Don't pump him out, don't pump him out.' I thought to myself I want to pump him out a little bit because he's got too much this morning. The judges said he made some mistakes and they said one time he didn't back. They said the other dog was standing on a wooded terrace and ole Bud was running so fast and came up on him so soon that he just jumped over him and didn't stop. That performance was one of the most fun things I have ever seen in my life. Peck Kelly came by me one time and said, 'You know, I sho' wish I didn't have to scout this other dog because I sho' would like to look at yours some more.' We got halfway through it and Bud was hot, just a jumping and a runnin'. I got him off to the side and he had got to where he wasn't minding me so good, so I got off my horse and cut me a switch and tapped him on the leg a few times, rubbed him down, and gave him a little water. After that we kinda got things back together and if you will read the Field he came back in the last hour and a half and made no mistakes. He jumped over the paved road at the end, and if I'm not mistaken, that dog had three finds in the last twenty minutes. When we picked him up there was some fella sitting there on a horse who was drunk, but not too drunk to know what he was looking at, say, 'White Lightning, hot damn!' I put him in a harness and he was still jumping and ready as I started down the road. Paul Walker had picked his dog up and Paul came riding down through there, looked at that ole dog for about ten minutes, and said, 'I'll tell you one thing, if I had him, I'd send everything else I got home.' I just can't describe to you the way that puppy was running. Clyde Morton had looked at him at the National Derby Championship and said, 'Well, he won't be a three-hour dog as he is not wide enough in the chest.' He won the Free-for-All right after that and Clyde said, 'I guess I was wrong.'

"A memory that comes to my mind is a setter, Flaming Starr," John Rex Gates stated. "We were running in the Saskatchewan Championship at Leon Covington's place and Flaming Starr came out there and was turned loose about eleven o'clock. It was running about one hundred degrees when he was turned loose. When Herman Smith turned him loose, he turned him into about a thirty-mile-an-hour wind. That dog just ate up the prairie. He was so determined that Mr. Herman couldn't catch him to give him a drink of water. He had several finds and won that Championship going away. For a setter, or any dog on that hot day, to go through there the way that dog did, and do it right in every way, was just remarkable."

When considering which dogs from the 1960s and 1970s that have the most impact on dogs today, Billy Morton replied, "White Knight, that's where it all started. That's where Ferrell Miller started his breeding program. I still think you see some of ole Bud's characteristics in dogs today. The dog I dearly loved was Armond Smart Alec. I wish you could have seem him the first summer we had him. That summer was his first year running all age. I didn't think we would ever get him broke. You could run him two or three hours and then that afternoon you could go back with him again if you wanted to. That dog could fly and find birds. Mary Oliver came up there that summer. She said that she wanted to raise some good puppies and didn't know what to breed to. Ole Alec was sitting out there by his barrel with his lip hanging down and she said in typical Mary Oliver fashion, 'Oh, I wouldn't breed to that ugly thing.' I told her what let's do. You get in that jeep and you get behind us when I turn him loose and I'm going to change your tune. He got out there and had about four or five finds and knocked several of them. When we arrived back at the house she started discussing breeding with Hoyle. When he won the Free-for-All he hadn't eaten in about three days because of kidney trouble. Hoyle thought about it and decided to turn him loose. It was about the gutsiest performance I ever saw a dog do. He died not long after that. He was the sire of Allure. I always wanted to breed him to Wrap Up but I never could get that done. There was a sister to Wrap Up who Dick Brown had for sale. I borrowed two hundred-fifty dollars, bought her, and bred her to Wrap Up. There was six or seven puppies in that litter. They all made good dogs. Every one of 'em that didn't make a running dog made a shooting dog."

Andy Daugherty agreed. "Most likely the dog that has had the most influence is Riggins White Knight. More fine dogs today probably go back to him than any other dog. I really liked the Rebel dogs in that same generation. Fred Arant had a good breed of dogs, the Rebel line, that he started himself. Their blood is still prominent in dogs that are running today. Funseeker's Rebel goes back to the Rebel line. The Rebel dogs were very workable and most generally good class bird dogs and would run when asked."

Addition's Go Boy and Fiddler had a huge impact according to Garland Priddy. "I think if you look at John Thompson's work, comparing the percentage of winners produced against the number of puppies whelped. These two dogs were well ahead of the others. Some dogs had more winners, but they had a tremendous amount of puppies produced. Go Boy goes back to A Rambling Rebel, which had a great impact on the breed. Millers Chief produced a lot of winners but he had a large amount of puppies. I think that Go Boy and Fiddler added run and bottom to their pups, and don't forget that they were both tremendous bird dogs. Go Boy was a natural front running dog but he didn't just run, he ran to find birds. If he was running down an edge and he picked up slight scent he would not leave the edge and go into woods two hundred yards, point the covey, and get buried up where we couldn't find him. He would continue down the edge looking for another covey. There are a still a few straws of frozen semen left of Addition's Go Boy. Of course Go Boy's Shadow was one of his offspring but was the opposite type of dog. He was big running but when he would catch scent of a bird he would go in looking for it. He might be buried up twenty minutes while we looked for him which often took him out of consideration.

One thing that might have held Go Boy's Shadow back a bit was that he was the type of dog that might have hunted too much."

Carrying on today, John Rex Gates replied, "I would have to say the Farrell Miller dogs. There's a ton of the white dogs out there. It took me a while to be convinced of that but they are still coming through today."

The question was what performance do you remember the most of a dog you were handling. "I've been very lucky in my life," Andy Daugherty recounted, "and I've had several what I would call real first-class performances by my dogs. Bear Creek Bess had such fine performances on the prairie and was a first class prairie dog. One of the best performances of my dogs was the Gunpowder dog at the Continental. When I picked him up I didn't think he was beatable there. I thought he did a tremendous job; he had seven finds, looked good and ran a remarkable dog race. Freddie Epp also told me it was one of the best performances he had seen. "

"The performance I remember so well," John Rex Gates proudly recalled, "was Oklahoma Flush in the Oklahoma championship. I had the second course in the afternoon, which was big open country. Butch was the type of dog that would run all over the world. And if he didn't hang up on birds, he would show back up in front of you. I was letting him roll through some of the pastures; he was going straight out of site and then would come back. There is a big hill on the course. When we rode to the top of that hill and looked on the far end of it, there he stood looking like who tied the bear. We called point a good half a mile from him, he was so proud of himself standing out there. We started a slow canter toward him. I didn't want to go fast because I wanted to show him off. In field trials you have got to put on a show. So we just started toward him and when we got there he must have had twenty prairie chicken in front of him. They started peeling off that hill one at a time. That was his first find. After that there was a barbed-wire fence surrounding a pasture of which there was only one way in and out. I sent him in there and he went plum out of sight. He went up on a hill and I knew he would come back if he didn't point birds. I had never seen any birds pointed in that pasture. I just wanted to send him through there, rare back on my horse and say, 'There he goes,' to the judges. He started back to us and upon exiting I shot him to the front with about ten minutes left to go. After a short period of time, about a half mile to the front, we saw him standing behind another covey of birds. The judges then said you can put the lead on him. Dr. Hawthorne used to put on that trial. He came up to me after the brace and said that they could run to this time next year and they won't beat you. The two judges and I were all grinning like a mule eating briars.

"Another great performance I remember like yesterday was at the Border International one year. I had the top five dogs in it. The judges came to me and wanted to know how to separate the dogs. I told them that I couldn't do it and that they were going to have to decide. Oklahoma Flush, The Texas Squire, Texas Allegheny Pete, The Company, and I believe Safari."

Billy Morton tells of the time when Wrap Up beat Oklahoma Flush in the Free-for-All. "It was just a good performance out of everyone, handlers and scouts. After the first hour I believe John Rex had four and I think I had two finds. That day it seemed that every bird she pointed was dead in front of her and all you had to do was walk right out there and pick them up. About an hour and a half later she made a huge swing through what we called the oat field. We then lost sight of her. After a while I sent Man in there and in a little while he called point and I got the birds up. Bill Brown was reporting that trial. Someone asked Bill after that find, 'Well, how have you got 'em now?' He said, 'Both dogs are about dead even.' I went on and I think I had about six more and John Rex was having a little trouble finding birds and I was getting them pretty regular. He rode by me and said, 'Boy, you pointing birds, aren't you.' You know in the Free-for-All, you can kill a bird if you trust your dog enough. Abut fifteen minutes to go she had a good find and I said it's about time. I got off and kinda stretched my shoulders a bit because I meant to kill a bird. I bet you I missed that bird four foot! She just stood there her tail and head a little higher and the hair kinda standin' up on her back. A very short time later she had another good find and it was a thing with Clyde Morton that you killed a cock bird if you could. I saw a cock bird swing to the left and I killed it, touched her on the head, and she went ov'a there and picked up the bird, came back, raided up on me, and handed me the bird. I knew school was out then. She did a whale of a job that day. Bill Brown was the best reporter and knew the most about dogs that I had ever seen. He came up to me after the brace and told me that he had always considered the best performance he had seen over three hours was Medallion and Palamonium. He then said, 'Let me tell you something. I've been going over it in my mind, and I don't know that the performance of these two dogs today to be the best I have ever seen.' "

"There are three that I can't separate," Garland Priddy stated. One was in Canada at the Saskatchewan that Go Boy won. He had four finds and stretched it out as far as he could go. One could have not have sketched it out better on a piece of paper. Second, was Mack's Realfoot Chief when he won the Continental in 1991 with seven finds. Thirdly, Go Boy's Shadow in the National Amateur. It was either 1990 or 1991. It snowed about eighteen inches. They held up two days and when they turned loose the third day there was still fifteen or sixteen inches of snow on the ground. He ran the hour and a half. He was liver and white and could be seen at a great distance. At pick up time he went out of sight; he was found by the scout in a draw with a covey of wild birds. He was the only dog that finished in the snow. A dog that ran when the snow melted won, but I thought that was as an outstanding a performance as I have ever seen. Everyone at the trial could not believe he went through the snow like he did."

When asked what the best advice ever received regarding training dogs was, Billy Morton guessed it was what his daddy told him. "Patience and live with them. My dogs lived with me and went everywhere with me. At one time I had two National Champions and an Amateur Champion sitting on the couch with me: Allure,

Wrapup, and Pandora. When I would open the door to let one out, the others would slide down next to me."

"I sat around and listened to a lot of the best trainers in the world when I was young," replied Andy Daugherty. "I listened to Leon Covington, who was a tremendous dog man, tell good stories, and I listened to Fred Arant, who told me 'When you raise a litter of puppies, the first thing you see that you don't like about a pup, give him to somebody. This way you will end up with a tremendous dog, maybe not in that litter, but you'll find one.' Jack Harper asked me one day at the National, 'Have you got your dogs handling good? They've got to handle at the National. That is the main thing at the national, they have got to listen.' I used to love to watch Dean Lord run shooting dogs, I thought he was a fantastic handler. When I was young I learned a lot by watching John Rex. One thing about it, I like to watch and learn. I don't think anyone ever gets too old to watch and learn."

John Rex Gates was very specific regarding the question. "Plan ahead, do your homework, know your courses that you are running on in a trial and your bird location. Even when pen-raised birds are released, they are usually released in about the same place each year. You need to know your courses and be prepared to get our dog in position. Plan ahead where you are going to put your dog down, where you hope to be at pick up time and all in between. Always show your dog to his best advantage in trials. Clyde Morton taught me this about showing a dog. When you are showing a dog in completion, take your horse and pull him up to a stop out in front of the gallery, turn the horse sideways to the gallery, look at them, and say, 'There he goes, judges.' That way you get their attention. Showmanship is a very important thing in field trials. First, you have got to have the right dog and next you have got to have some showmanship. If you can feel good about what you are doing yourself and can convert that over to the judges, then you are a step ahead."

"Fred Arant was my mentor and gave me this advice," Garland Priddy said thoughtfully. "Our grounds on the prairie overlapped and we would visit with each other from time to time. Fred told me this sitting in his camp one day. He said that anybody can break a dog on birds but you have got to spend effort and time on the ground pattern. I followed that. The dogs that were not naturally front-running dogs, we worked very hard on them. I thought that was the best piece of information that anybody ever gave me."

"I worked with my dad and went around the country with him until 1982. He was not only my dad but my mentor," Andy Daugherty said with pride. "I learned a lot from him. He would holler at me and tell me what I should have done and what I should have not done. You didn't have to worry about knowing when he was mad at you; he was very frank about it. He always took tremendous care of his dogs and did everything to make sure his dogs were in good shape. You can try any angle you please, he would say, but there was no substitute for work. Not only did he say that, he lived it. We worked in conditions that nobody would have worked. Back then you didn't think about not going to train, if he was going, then you were going. He taught me how to run the business end and how to handle people. This has been a lifelong deal for me, and I have enjoyed every minute of it. If you stay in this—Dad relayed this to me—you will have down years when nothing works right in a field trial. Then, the next year your luck turns and you can flush birds on the highway."

"When I was just a kid, Daddy would always have a couple of litters of puppies around. My mother would meet me at after school with some dogs in the trunk, drop me off, and I would take the puppies hunting," Billy Morton recalled. "I always go back to what Daddy, my mentor, taught me about patience. Don't get in a big rush. These puppies will break themselves if you find enough birds. I would break them and we would sell them the next year. There was a fellow that called Daddy from Texas and told him he wanted a dog that would do something that the others won't do. He wanted a dog that would go out and pick a bird up by his head and never put his mouth on his body. He told Daddy that he would pay five hundred dollars for a dog like that. I had a puppy Daddy had given me the year before out of ole Greenwood Bill. When the man said five-hundred dollars, I told Daddy that I believed I could do that. I had already yard broke him. I thought and thought and finally I got a big ole glass jug that was big enough that he couldn't get his mouth around it to pick it up. I got me some bird feathers and stuck 'em around the mouth of the jug. I could roll the jug out and the only way the puppy could bring it back to me was to pick it up by the feathers in the end. That fall, the first bird I killed I sent him out there and he picked it up by the head and brought it back to me. We sent him on to the man and he was tickled to death with the dog. He called back later and said, 'I want one more dog like ole Bill' and I said, 'Yes, sir, I do too!' I remember the first time I went to the National, which was 1945, horses were renting for ten dollars a day. Daddy scraped up the ten dollars and let me ride that morning and he rode that afternoon. I came back and told my daddy that I sure would like to win this thing one day. He looked at me and said, 'You've got to get a lot more patience than you've got right now.' I walked around a minute thinking about what he said and spied Mississippi Zeb, who had already run. I walked over there and rubbed him and played with him for a few minutes and eventually he won it that year.

"We put in a lot of hard work," John Rex Gates said rather forcefully. "I grew up under my dad and mentor, John S. Gates. He was quite a trainer himself. I started handling the horses and dog wagon when I was six or seven years old out on that prairie. He would always give me dogs to check cord. If we busted up some chickens, he would tell me, 'Boy, you watch those chicken down and take a dog over there and work those dogs. If you fool with these dogs enough, you'll learn to read them. You've got to get in their head when you are working a dog. When you are working them, they'll teach you more than anybody can ever teach you.' He taught me the ethic of hard work. He said, 'Buddy, you've got to plan ahead and work your plan the best you can. If you ever lose your temper working a dog, you go immediately and pick up that dog and put him in the kennel and don't turn him out again until you get over your hot spell. You can actually ruin a dog in one or two minutes of anger and do more harm than you can ever bring back.' He used to tell us that if you have got to go to the bathroom, you had better go at night because we ain't got time in the day. Freddie Epp went with us and so did Garland Davis. My dad used to have a scout named Peck Kelly. He is probably one of the best scouts there has ever been in the world. My dad used to say something about Peck that was remarkable. He said Peck could track a dog down a blacktop road and could identify an individual dog's track. That's the way Peck used to find most of those dogs, He'd track 'em."

Billy Morton shared memories of the early days. "I scouted for Hoyle Eaton the first year he trained down at Canton, Mississippi. That was the year that White Knight was a derby. Both of us were green, and Jack Harper would come down there once or twice a week to look in on us. He really helped us more than anybody. The best part I can remember is that Hoyle was paying me fifteen dollars a week and I was drawing twenty-one dollars unemployment compensation. I would drive back to Booneville, Mississippi, in a '48 Ford. You had to love it. We would work from daylight until after dark. Hoyle always had a lot of patience with dogs. He would not fly into a dog but would give them the benefit of the doubt. We didn't have any running water or any bathrooms in the house we lived in the first year, everything was froze up. It was really cold in that little house. I told him that if we don't quit now we never will. If it hadn't have been for White Knight that first winter when it was so cold, I think I would have froze to death. Ole Bud and a little setter slept with me, they were about the warmest things I had around there."

Man Rand was unquestionably one of the best, if not the best scout that ever rode. Billy Morton was quick to tell this story on the famed scout. "We didn't have electric collars and that stuff and I was real fortunate that I had Man Rand, who is in the Field Trial

Hall of Fame. Man was one of the best scouts I have ever seen. I have seen him look down on a sand road, pick up his dogs tracks over others and see which way he was going. He was a real good horseman. The best story on Man was a day when we were braced with Marshall Loftin at the Free-for-All and doing a whale of a good job. Marshall had an old bitch who wouldn't back; this wasn't the first time we had been braced with her. After about two hours, Man called point and I got there first and saw Man on the ground. Here came that old bitch and we both knew she was going to knock the birds. Man followed her and tackled her before she could get to the birds. Marshall ran up and said, "Man, what are you doing to my dog?" Man told him, "She done taken my money over in Mississippi and she ain't going to take it here!"

Each of these trainers were asked if they felt they trained in the golden age of field trials. Their answers showed a true reverence for the sport, an insight on friendship and a hope for tomorrow.

"Oh yeah, there is no question about that!" Billy Morton said with zeal. "We didn't have electric collars and had to go out there and do things the hard way. We didn't rush dogs. There was Hoyle Eaton, John Gates, Howard Kirk, Paul Walker, Fred Arant, Jack Harper, who was one of the finest trainers who has ever been, all of them. At that time all these trainers had truly great dogs. Back then a young man starting out could count on help from the other trainers. It was a family affair. I met so many nice people. Years ago it wasn't nothing for four or five of us, and White Knight, to stay in a room together. At Paducah, Kentucky, if you turned Bud out in the spring he would go back to the room he had stayed in in the fall and wait for you. It would usually be me, Hoyle, Tommy Olive, and others in the room. In the night when ole Bud wanted to go out, all of us would wait on the other one to let the dog out. That old dog would get a boot in his mouth and would start hitting you on the head and would go down the line until he would find someone who would get up and let him out. He knew you had to put the boot on to go outside, that's sense! I loved that ole dog."

"Yes sir, I do. I think the Golden age may be passing us." Andy Daugherty remembered the training in the sixties and seventies when there were wild birds everywhere he went. "Now we have some trials where we throw birds out and a dog has to get right on them to smell, can get within six inches of them and they still sit there. Now this is the best they've got and the people who are putting these trials on are doing a tremendous job but it's not like it was in the sixties. Now we have to use training devices like electric collars. Back then we could just wait five minutes and point another covey. If your dog made a mistake then you could get on him, wait five minutes, and point another covey. He would forget about the mistake and you getting on to him and you could start fresh when contacting another covey."

"I do," replied Garland Priddy. "I think I saw the last couple of decades of the golden age of field trials. Especially All Age as I can't speak for the others. We have lost grounds and I see us possibly losing more. Another detriment is the decline of the bird populations in many areas of the United States. There are not the birds for new people to get started on."

John Rex Gates possibly summed it up the best. "I think any of the years were golden to anybody who trained and loved bird dogs. The Lord has blessed me. What was so good about the era I trained was that we had plenty of ground to work on. There were still the hedge rows and quail were everywhere. The Canadian prairie was still open and not fenced up a lot or plowed like it's beginning to be now. Back then, as a general rule, most of the dogs were bigger running dogs than they are today because they had more country to cover. It was a great time to be working dogs in the sixties and seventies. Back then, all the trainers tried to help each other. I think that is also done today. In the trials, the completion was tough because we had such a great bunch of handlers and trainers. Bud and Andy Daugherty, Fred Arant Jr., Hoyle Eaton, Freddy Epp, Bill and Freddie Rail, Garland Priddy, George Morland, Leon Covington in his later years, Howard Kirk, Herman and Collier Smith, and others. We would normally all meet up at the bigger trials and everyone had good dogs."

Dogs and trainers will come and go as life is fragile and fleeting. There are still memories to make and exciting braces are to be run. It is important to remember the events, dogs, and personalities that have paved the way for us to enjoy this sport we so love. By doing so, we can deepen our enjoyment of the present and anticipate a bright future.

Andy Daugherty
Photo courtesy of Andy Daugherty

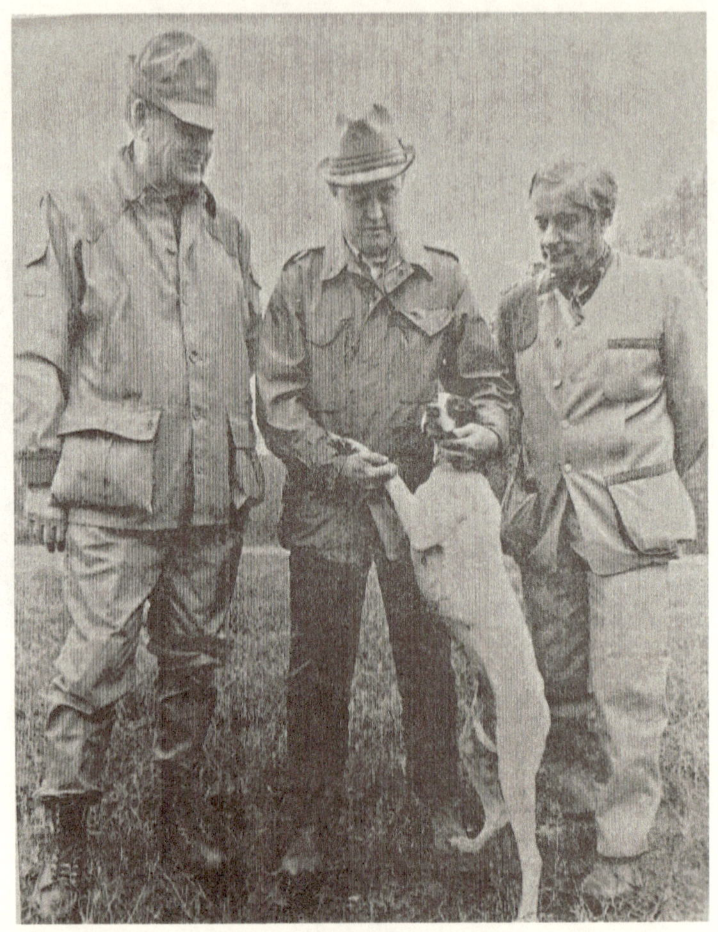

Paul "Bear" Bryant, Billy Morton and Curt Gowdy with Wrapup

Photo courtesy of The Selma Times-Journal

Billy Morton with Ben "Man" Rand in front of the Big House at Sedgefields Plantation with Pandora, Wrapup and Allure
Photo courtesy of Billy Morton

Garland Priddy with Go Boy's Frozen Addition
Photo courtesy of Garland Priddy

John Rex and Robin Gates at a Canadian prairie trial
Photo courtesy of John Rex Gates

The Era of the Scout

They rode like the wind and could handle horses like a cowboy. Always out there but seldom seen. Often with unmatched eyesight, hearing, and an uncanny ability to turn the impossible into the possible during a field trial. Trackers, trainers, horseman, and one of a kind: these were the scouts of the middle 1950s through much of the 1970s. This time in the field trial world can be called many things, but this author choses to call it the "Era of the Scout."

Eyesight, having an inbred instinct of knowing where a dog was, and being good at bringing out the best qualities of a dog all describe Robert Burris. Perhaps the best description of Robert may be from the dictionary. Loyalty is devotion and faithfulness to a cause, group, or person. Above all, Robert was loyal.

Hoyle Eaton had told his friend Dick Brown that he needed a helper. "He knew Robert and his family and told me to go out there and see Robert Burris. So I went to his place and there was nineteen-year-old Robert. He worked for me for about three years and then went north and worked for the railroad for a couple of years. And then one Christmas morning I heard someone knocking at the door and it was Robert. He said, 'Mr. Hoyle, would you take me back and hire me?' And I said I would. That's how he got started with me."

Robert had a special gift to be able to think like a dog. He scouted many famous dogs, White Knight and Red Water Rex possibly being the best of the bunch. To Robert's credit, he knew exactly what to do and was one of the best at showing the dog he was scouting. The work was never too hard nor the weather too cold or hot for him not to be on the line, happy to turn a dog loose. He was rather quiet and well-liked by the other handlers, scouts, and the people in the gallery.

In preparation for his first scouting assignment, Mr. Eaton told this story on Robert. "I was at Canton, Mississippi, at the time training White Knight. Billy Morton was my scout. I told Robert, who was wanting to start scouting, to get out there and watch Man Rand, Peck Kelly, and the others and try to pick up on some things you will need to know. So he went out and rode a half a day. Then that afternoon he didn't want to go back out. I asked him why he didn't want to go back out, and he said that he had learned all he needed to know that morning! Later, after realizing just what it took to scout, he laughed at himself for saying that."

David Johnson knew Robert well. "Robert was very good with dogs and had a special way with them. When you were scouting against him, he was very tough completion. He knew his dogs and most always knew where they were. With the caliber of dogs that Robert was working and scouting, he had to know his dogs and know where to go and find them. I think he could turn his dogs loose and not pay them any attention and then know where to go to find the dog or the dog would come to him." John Rex Gates said he was a "dang good scout" and Freddie Rayl thought "he was a very good scout in every way."

Hoyle Eaton shared this story, "We were running White Knight in the Invitational at Paducah. This happened on the run-off. Everything was froze hard as a rock that morning. There was a creek that ran parallel to the course. White Knight had somehow got across the creek. The further the creek went the wider and deeper it got. The course eventually turned away from the creek. White Knight was getting the job done but could not cross. Robert got White Knight, put him in the saddle, and off into the icy creek he went. Robert let him out on the other side of the creek in front of me and he went on to win the trial. The creek was deep enough his horse had to swim a little bit and Robert got wet and extremely cold but finished the brace."

Another memory Mr. Eaton shared was when they were working dogs on the prairie. "I went one way and Robert went the other. When I caught up to him, Robert was running around and around a bluff. I thought to myself what is going on, what is he doing? When I got there, I heard a dog fighting with something. When I found the dog, he had a hold of a porcupine. I asked Robert why he didn't go in there and see what the matter was. He said, 'I ain't about to go in there. I thought it was a lion or a tiger."

Robert died in his late forties of pneumonia. Billy Morton fondly remembered what happened at his burial. "He was to be buried at a little church out in the country. When the mourners started out to the grave to bury him, there was a covey of quail dusting in the dirt, which had been dug for his grave. As the people approached the birds took flight." A fitting tribute to a man who loved dogs and trialing.

"Joe Bush worked for Harold Ray when he was a boy cleaning kennels as similar tasks," Freddie Rayl remembered. "Harold called my dad and told him that he had a young boy working for him who wanted to go north and do you need anybody to go with you? My dad was the type of man who wouldn't tell anyone no. So he told Harold if he wanted to go, he would be glad to take him if he truly wanted to learn the business and learn about dogs. Harold lived about one hundred sixty miles from us, and back then it was about ninety percent dirt roads. Joe rode the whole way in the back of Harold's truck and was literally caked in dust when he arrived at our house. When he got out, he had a big ole smile on his face. which is one thing Joe pretty much had all the time.

"Joe was not only a tremendous scout but was one of the first, if not the first, African-American handlers to run a dog in a major All Age stake. He had a very nice dog called Meadow Brook Joe that he ran himself and did a fair amount of winning. He won the International Pheasant Championship and won a couple of all age championships with him. He qualified and ran him in the National. I scouted for him when Meadow Brook Joe won. I guess I was the one that broke the ice by allowing a black scout to run a dog in his string. Sometimes I was criticized for it, but it was my call. I've always been my own man and the only one who could tell me very much was my dad," said Freddie Rayl.

Excited about the interview, Mr. Bush stated, "When I went to Canada, I was fifteen years old. I went up there with Mr. Bill Rayl. Those all age dogs could really run and I fell in love with them. I had never seen a dog run so far. Most of what I learned about scouting I learned from Mr. Bill and Freddie Rayl. Mr. Bill was one of the best trainers I ever saw. He would work and work a dog and would stay out there until he got it right. If he was working a dog, even if he had to walk beside a horse, he would keep him out there all morning or all day to get him straight. I'm telling you he could really train a dog. He didn't go out in search of trained or almost-trained dogs, and he didn't mind doing the work himself. Mr. Bill always made our dogs. He really knew how to put a pattern and a finishing touch on a dog. Back in those days you had to have two or three horses to chase running dogs down in an hour."

According to Freddie Rayl, he had "an uncanny knack of finding lost dogs—that was probably his best quality. Joe had an incredible set of hawk-like eyes on him. He could spot a dog or anybody or anything from way off, he could see somebody coming a mile away and tell you who it was and what color horse he was riding when all everyone else could see was a blur. He was just an incredible scout and scouted for me on a lot of my champion dogs. I won fifty-two championships and over seventy runner-ups, and he scouted most of them."

John Thompson remembered clearly, “If he ever got to one of Mr. Fred’s dogs, he could set him up and you would think he was etched in stone. He was an expert at yard-working a dog when the dog was young. He could style a dog up and walk all around the dog without the dog losing a bit of style. If a dog ever started to crouch a little, he would take his knife and bump that rascal on the back leg and make him stand up. If the dog ever turned his head, he would bump him on the head with his knife. I guarantee you that if Joe got to a dog on point first, and called point, by the time you got to him he would look like a bull before his first fight.”

Freddie Rayl felt like he had a second nature and bond with the dogs he scouted. “Yeah, yeah, He had had a bond with the dogs. That’s one of the reasons he could find a dog so well. He had an uncanny knack of thinking like a dog and knowing where he would go and what he would do.”

John Thompson relayed, “He could put a dog on birds like nobody else. I guarantee you that if he rode up some birds he could put a dog on ’em like he had them on a string. He was an artist at that.”

“He was real good with bad horses,” according to Freddie Epp. “He could stay on them until they were better horses. He could break pretty wild horses and make them humble. He was always very aware of the things going on around him and he could tell you where your dog was even if he was running in the brace against you. He helped me a lot of times, and I’d say he was a pretty talented fellow.”

David Johnson told this story on his friend Joe Bush: “We were up in Paducah, Kentucky, at the Invitational and he was riding a young horse. The horse didn’t know much about crossing ditches and big mud puddles. There was a fairly small mud puddle. When the horse got to it, he looked down and saw his reflection in the water and it spooked him. He tried to jump it and when he did his foot slipped and he turned a flip with Joe, and hit the mud puddle and just dried it out with him. It was very cold, and in just a little bit his clothes just froze up on him. He kept going even though he was very cold."

"I think I really got along with all the other scouts well. It seemed that David and I bumped heads a lot in a good way. When I was around a field trial, I tried to help everybody. I never went out half way I, went out and tried out one hundred percent. I helped a bunch of folks win championships: Mr. Bill Hunt, Mr. Tom Honecker, Randy Anderson. I didn't go out there like some people talking and looking all around, I went out there to win," said Joe Bush.

Joe especially wanted to recognize Harold Ray and Sherry Ebert for their work with the setters. "Anybody that could do what they did with their dogs had to be a first-class trainer. Mr. Harold would put out a pigeon line and then work his dogs on them. He was a master at styling up dogs using this.

"Probably the best dog I ever scouted was Fiddler's Addition." Joe Bush's voice rose with excitement. "Mr. Bill Ball started him. He then sold him to Mr. Ted Baker and Mr. T.J. Robinson. He was an awesome dog. We lost several championships right at pick up time as that joker would go out there so far. When he got on point, he was there. When we would hit him with that whistle, he would go and get in that country. Hot weather, cold weather, he could cut it. It could be a hundred degrees out there and that son of a gun could do it up."

The greatest performances Joe Bush witnessed by a dog were Fiddler at the Invitational championship and Sean Derrig's dog, Tin Soldier, at the International Pheasant Championship. "I just rubbed my head. That joker ran through that country. O-hoo, o-hoo, he looked awfully good. Fiddler's Addition's brother, Fiddler's Free Boy, wasn't a slouch either. He could point wild birds but he really loved liberated birds. He could point those son of a guns. He could really sock it to them. When he won the Masters Championship, the wind was probably blowing about seventy miles per hour. This trial was on wild birds. He went through there pointing those birds, oh man. His first two years, I think we lost him in every trial. We never could finish him. I kept working with him and said I've got to figure him out. I kept steadying and steadying him. I noticed that when I was leading him to the line to start a field trial, he would get to shaking all over, and when I turned him loose, he would haul it and never look back. So I took my spike collar off my saddle and any time I would lead him to the line, I put that spike collar on him. With that spike collar, he settled down and after that we stopped losing him and started winning with him."

The Florida Open and the Continental were Joe's favorite trials to scout. "I loved the Continental, so did everyone else. A dog has to be tough there and every jump a dog makes he has got to be hunting. A dog can run up on birds anywhere, even at the breakaway. Those birds can be anywhere down there. I did not worry about my dogs running an hour at these trials. They could run an hour and reach back and then get some more."

David Johnson perhaps summed up Joe Bush the best. "He was my toughest competition. When he went to a trial, he went to win."

Upright and honest, respectful, not a showman, good around people, and all business. These are just a few of David Johnson's traits that were repeated over and over. When asked what he thought were the traits of a good scout, David replied, "A good scout has to be real good about finding a dog. You never want to boost your ego but rather stay on the sideline. A scout is not there to be a show. To be a good scout, you have got to know your dogs well. A scout has to have the knack to figure out a dog, to take anybody's dog and do well with them." This was David Johnson's philosophy in a nutshell.

"David was raised within five miles of us," John Rex Gates recalled. "He came over and asked for work and we started him off, like everyone else, cleaning the kennels. He then started going to the field with us, and he just picked up on it. He had a natural quality to work with dogs. I remember the first time he called point for us. We were in Canada and he was a long way from us, standing on the saddle, waving at us. He said by standing up in the saddle we would know the dog was on point because he and the horse were not moving."

"One year at the Dominion trial"—as told by Freddie Epp—"his horse fell with him and broke his arm. He went on and finished the brace without complaining or quitting."

"He was an accomplished horseman. He could really ride," according to John Thompson. "He, like all the other good scouts, could really concentrate on a dog. David always kept the dog he was scouting in sight but would never ride him down. He was very good at steadying dogs and it took a shore 'nuff outlaw to get away from him. It seemed he had a second sense about him as to which way the dog was going to go. He was always thinking while he was running a dog. If there was a mud hole, he would look for tracks and see which way the dog was going. He knew what his dogs tracks looked like."

Luke Weaver shared, "During my career in field trials, David Johnson was the best scout I ever saw. He was, and still is, a class act. He was a great rider. I saw him ask someone in the gallery to lead a horse for him to swap out during the brace. He came through, jumped off his horse to the other horse, and his feet never hit the ground."

John Thompson remembered two instances of David's special scouting ability. "I was judging the trial and he was scouting Special Beauty. She could get away from you in a heartbeat. After two finds, she went off left in the woods to the front and I said, 'Well she got away from him this time.' John Rex just kept on riding as if nothing was wrong. It was right at thirty minutes when I turned her over to the other judge. After about fifteen minutes, we met and I asked the judge how it went and he said, 'I don't know how he did it but he found that dog. That dog was a mile and a half away.' Secondly, I was judging a trial in Canada and Bill Hunt was running Crossbow. That dog was running big and faded out of sight to the front. I said to myself, 'he won't get him' as he couldn't ride straight to the front. We went on to some sand dunes and the course turned about ninety degrees to the right. There was a lake that must have been a mile and a half or two miles away. Before we got off the dunes, we had to turn sharp back to the right again. When we started to turn right, that dog came running down a fence line right straight ahead of us. I looked over toward the lake and you could just see David. He was like an ant it was so far. How he got that dog that far off and turned him back to the front I don't know."

"David could take a short running dog and slip him around, point birds with him, or shoot him out front a half mile in front, which would make you think he was running all over everything. He was the best of this," said Freddie Rayl.

"He had a great memory and his hearing is the best of any scout I've ever seen," stated Luke Weaver. "Bubba Moreland was running a dog with me in the Free-for-All. I thought she was gone when David came up to me. He said, 'She ain't lost, I hear her.' It must have been ten minutes from the time he said that until Bubba came back with the dog. I don't see how in the world he head him that far. He was a great trainer. He helped train a lot of those dogs and he was a great horseman. He was just really just a class act."

Palariel Stormy Clown was David's favorite dog to scout. "Back in the day when there were dogs that would really run, I loved to watch him," David shared. "He was the type of dog when you were out scouting you did not have to worry about hooking back. He always stayed on the front end and would go through the country well. He would run as much as the country would let him, and was a super nice bird dog. He was the type dog that whenever he stands the higher he gets. And that ole head would just stay up there. If it come a hard rain I believe he would drown."

When asked what was the finest performance of a dog you witnessed, David did not hesitate. "I would say that I loved watching Kansas Wind up on the prairies. He was a dog that would hang out there as far as the eye can see. You did not have to worry about losing him because he would always find you."

Joe Bush related a great story on David. "At Lake City, Florida, he was flipped over a fence and his horse fell on him and he could not get up. He said all he could do was call point. He knew they would come a running if he called point. The judges and gallery came looking for the dog on point and he called, 'I'm down here on the ground.' They found him with the horse laying on top of him and they had to roll the horse off him. He said, 'One thing about it, if you call point, somebody will come a riding!'

His favorite grounds to scout were the Continental and the Masters when it was run at Blue Springs. "The grounds for the Masters and the Continental were similar. They were perfect for a dog and it was easy to get a dog around. Mr. Ted Baker's grounds were nice. I used to really enjoy going down there."

David was very proud that he has scouted 123 championships. "I think that is a very good record and to my knowledge I am ahead of everyone else." He still trains with Fred Robinson in Tennessee and makes a few trials. Perhaps a fitting ending for this section is a quote from David himself: "I have really enjoyed everyone I have met and everywhere I have gone with bird dogs."

To say that Loren (Peck) Kelley was a superb horseman was an understatement. John Rex Gates remembered, "When I was a kid, I used to go lead horses for some of the big field trials. I would lead Peck's scouting horses. Peck would tell me that when he would come through the gallery to throw the reins over the fresh horse and get out of the way, Peck would come along at a cantor and would jump from one horse to the next and go on about his business. He really was quite a showman. Freddie Rayl saw Peck Kelly when he was a young boy in the early sixties. "I remember seeing him have a person in the gallery lead usually three horses for him. When he left the gallery, he left wide open, and when he came back, he came back wide open. When he would return to the gallery, he would jump off one horse and mount another and leave wide open, he would do that the whole hour. He didn't lope and he didn't walk; he left in a dead run."

Peck started out as a cook at Mercer Mills Plantation for John Gates in the early 1940s. It is told that he was an accomplished cook and could cook almost anything. He started his career with dogs when he was seventeen or eighteen years old, traveling to the prairies with John Gates.

Dr. Sam Orr Black penned Peck's obituary in the Field. He wrote, "Peck Kelley was a high-type person, a superior horseman, and in my opinion was the best scout I ever saw work in field trials. He was gentlemanly, wore shell-rimmed glasses most of the time, and stuttered slightly when he tried to get words out too quickly." Peck made a lasting impact on the field trial world even though he died at the young age of thirty-seven in an automobile accident after delivering a pup to Pineland Plantation.

Hoyle Eaton remembered that Peck could "ride like the wind" and would lay out on the far side of a horse going across the prairies just to keep the judges from seeing him. "All you would see is a riderless horse going across the prairies." Nathan Cottrell took this subject a bit further. "I had a short running dog that I wanted to run in a field trial in Canada. I was braced with Camelot who John Gates ran. He was a pretty good running and tough dog. We were riding along and there was one bush up ahead maybe a half mile to a mile. When John and I got up to that bush, there was Peck Kelley behind it watering both dogs. I asked Peck, 'How did you get up here?' He replied, 'I hunkered down on the side of my horse like an Indian where nobody would see me.' He was straight in front at least a half a mile on the Canadian prairies and nobody knew he was there!" Mr. Cottrell added an important comment after telling this story. "Both John Gates and Peck were straight-up guys."

Mr. Cottrell continued, "He could do it all. He knew what to do and when to do it. As good a scout as I have ever seen. I had Peck Kelly help me one time and it was like you were playing on a Super Bowl team. He was so good all you had to do was ride along and do your job and never worry about him."

It was common knowledge that Peck and Man Rand were intense competitors and often would have situations arise between them. One would tell the other how his dog would beat the other's and the other would say "If you find my dog you had better take care of him. If you take care of mine I'll take care of yours."

An exceptional tracker, John Rex Gates remembers his dad saying that Peck would watch the crossings for tracks and could track a dog down a blacktop highway.

Peck was not without humor. At the National, when he was braced against White Knight as a derby, he rode by Billy Morton, who was scouting for Hoyle Eaton, and said, "I sho wish I didn't have to look at this ole dog of mine because I sho is enjoying looking at yours."

He was an important piece of the John Gates operation. Mr. Gates said Peck was his right arm. Not only scouting but helping in the training at Mr. Gates direction. Smart, good with the public, at times quiet, referred to more than once as a good guy, and an expert at slipping dogs to the front, Peck Kelly is remembered as one of the great horseman and scouts.

To say that Ben (Man) Rand was around dogs all his life is not an exaggeration. That's what helped him become an elite scout. He scouted for approximately six decades, scouted thirteen National Champions, nineteen National Free-for-All champions, eleven national Derby champions and ten American Field Futurity winners. He worked for Mr. Holloway before Clyde Morton came to Sedgefields. Billy Morton shared, "There was a big net-wire fence that went all the way around the big house and to the front gate. When Man was about nine or ten years old, his first job was to sit at the gate and keep the puppies from coming out. If he saw Mr. Sage or other visitors coming, he would open the gate for them. When you have thirty-five or forty puppies running loose and you are sitting there playing with them all day, you learn some things that other people would not even think about. I think that is what make Man so good with dogs—he lived with them." Jimmy Hinton said, "There was no one better with a puppy than Man."

He was a student of dogs and according to Freddie Epp, “Man sort of taught you to think like a dog.”

Sedgefields Plantation was where Man worked at and where he grew up. “That’s where you had to worry about Man the most,“ David Johnson remembered thoughtfully. “On his own grounds and up at Grand Junction, Tennessee, as those grounds were similar, it seemed like Man and his dogs would go from covey point to covey point. Man would wear you out at these trials.”

John Thompson once asked Man which dog was his favorite of the ones Mr. Clyde campaigned. He said, “Well, sir, I sorta liked Ariel. I liked him because when he got a little bit tired, he pointed straight ahead of me. You didn’t have to look for him.”

Man was a true woodsman and could sometimes to remarkable things. Clyde Morton would tell about Man carrying two sticks on his saddle with a big heavy bolt off a railroad track, flush chickens, and if he wanted one he would knock it down with one of those sticks to let a dog get his mouth on it in areas they couldn’t shoot. He never missed.

There was no question he was an amazing horseman. Billy Morton witnessed him. “At the National, when we lost a dog in some deep gullies. After he found the dog, he turned his horse up the bank which was too steep to ride, grabbed the horse’s tail to pull himself up, and when the horse came out, Man was on top of him.”

“He could just think like a dog. He could ride up to a field. He might not know which way that dog went or which way to go. It just looked like something was bred into him to know where the dog went in, he just knew that much about dogs.” Joe Bush remembered that he had the ability to put a dog anywhere he wanted.

“He was real good at yard-breaking dogs and puppies,” Billy Morton recounted. “In the big barn, there was a big hallway. Man would get puppies every morning, snap them, and play with them there. Then, when he started yard-breaking them, he had another snap he would put on their collars and a belt he would put underneath the dog to hold the dog up where the dog could never sit down. He had patience and he would just sit there and fool with them. He would work the puppies and when all of them would learn the lesson he was teaching, he would move them to the next step. He had a system and he always went by it. After the summer he had them where they would heel, retrieve, you could stop them in the yard, and make each pup come to him. I think that was one key to Clyde's dogs, they all were very obedient."

Some of Man's training techniques were unconventional. One technique Man used when gaining dominance over a hard-headed dog was to bite its ear. Billy Morton laughed when telling this story. "We had a big ole dog named Sam. I'll bet the dog weighed a hundred and ten pounds. He was very hard-headed. One day we were working him and he just wouldn't do anything we wanted him to do. I heard Man tell the dog that if he didn't behave he was going to bite his ear. In a little while I heard the dog scream. I headed in that direction and I could see something black appear out of the sage grass and then disappear. When I got there I realized what it was. Man had that dog's ear in his mouth and every time the dog would flip Man over his back, boots would appear over the sage grass. When they got thorough with the fight, I guarantee the dog could hear."

To say Man was superstitious is an understatement. Billy Morton told a story that backs this statement up. "We were traveling some backroads on the way to the Invitational in Kentucky. All of a sudden Man started hollering, 'Stop, stop!' I didn't know whether the trailer had torn up or what so I stopped real quick. I said, 'What is the matter, Man?' He said, 'A black cat just ran across the road. We can't cross over his path.' I asked him, 'What do you want me to do?' He said, 'We gotta turn around or we are going to be hexed and not win anything.' We got turned around and the cat crossed in front of us as we started to go the other way. I asked Man, 'What are we going to do now?' Man said that we could go ahead, as the cat had the hex on his back this time and not on his feet."

This was not the only case of Man being superstitious. One day he and Billy Morton were mowing some fields for a field trial with a couple of old tractors. They had moved into an area where they had to get off their tractors, and Billy remarked that there might be rattlesnakes in the area. Man got down on his knees and looked and sure enough there was one. After killing it, they went on with Billy on the lead tractor and Man following. While crossing an old bridge, it gave way on one side and threw Billy underneath. Man came down and dragged Billy out from under the tractor, and Billy thought he was going to ask him if he was hurt. But to his surprise, Man said, 'Mr. Billy, us is goin' to use up all our luck before we get to the field trial!' "

There are probably enough stories that happened among scouts to fill a book. One story goes that Man was to scout the first brace the next morning. The scouts were playing cards and wanted to get Man drunk so he would not be effective as a scout. They were passing a bottle around, making sure there was plenty in it when it was Man's turn to drink. Every time he got the bottle he would just kiss it and pour a bit of whiskey in his boot. He did this until the game broke up and the bottle was empty. When asked what he did with the whiskey in the boot he replied, "There was nothing wrong with it. I poured it in a bottle when I got to my room and drank it on a later date."

Man was confident in his abilities. John Thompson shared a story. "I asked Mr. Joe Hurdle what was the best performance he had seen at the National and he said Palamonium in 1959. He had thirteen or fourteen finds. The brace was almost over and Mr. Clyde told Mann, 'Don't you call point again, we don't need any more birds.' In a little bit the dog got out there and pointed. Soon as it happened Man said, 'Poooiiiiinnnnnttttttt! Got a point over here.' Mr. Clyde was fit to be tied. When he got to Man he stated in no uncertain manner, 'I told you not to call point anymore.' He didn't want the dog to have an unproductive. Man replied, 'There they sats right there in front of 'em." When later asked why his dogs didn't have many unproductives, he said, "Before I call point, I gets off the horse and looks." Freddie Epp backed this story up. "I asked Man why he didn't have many unproductives when he called point. He said, 'I get down and crawls right in front of the dog until I sees the birds and then I craws back out and calls point.' "

Before running a dog, Billy Morton once told Man, "The front belongs to me and the sides and the back belong to you. If you lose this dog, we won't make any money." "Yes, sir," he replied, "we ain't goanna lose him." Jimmy Hinton once said this about Man, "When I went to a field trial there was only one person I wanted to take, and that was Man." Man Rand was surely one of the greatest of all time.

Fred Arant didn't run what would be called "handling" dogs. Most of his dogs were live running and the only thing that would stop them was a bird or if Joe Odom turned them. Fred needed a scout who could go to the end of the world after a big running dog and bring them back to the front, and that was exactly what he found in Joe Odom. Joe was not over five feet tall, knock-kneed, and didn't look like he could hardly sit a horse much less ride one, but he could ride the heck out of one. John Rex Gates described him as "an artist in finding big running dogs and showing them." David Johnson said, "He was a master at slipping around with his dogs and shooting them out to the front." And Freddie Rayl commented that in his opinion, "Joe was the best of them all."

He could go anywhere and win. Not just at local trials but he could go to grounds he was not familiar with and do well. He had an uncanny knack of finding a dog, getting him back, and sending him across the front without anybody seeing him. Freddie Rayl explained, "Joe had to do quite a bit. He had to go hard and get the dog, slip around and then send him out around the front. I've seen him send one across the front and then go after him, chase him a mile or two and send him across the front again. Once a dog got to showing good and pointing a bird or two, Fred would go to working and handling the dog and helping Joe. He might have been different in his younger days, but when I saw him, he would hang with the judges and tell jokes and stories. I think that might have been a plan that he and Joe had worked up. Fred would tell jokes and distract the judges so Joe could get out there and do what Fred wanted and they wouldn't notice him. Joe was a bit different from the other scouts because everyone expected him to go and get all of Fred's dogs because that was the type of dogs he ran."

"Joe was helping John Rex run Fred's dogs at a trial because he was sick. One of the dogs was named Mission. The dog was doing a heck of a job and already had a couple of finds. He went across a big field and jumped over in tall cover on the side. Joe had a big ole bay horse that he rode for years. He wasn't over five feet tall and knock-kneed. You would think he would not even be able to sit a horse but he could ride the heck out of one. As he got to the edge, the horse started running away with him. As this happened, he saw Mission on point. He just reached down and grabbed the horse by the bit and pulled him around in a circle. He would raise his hat and call point and make a big circle and come back by the dog and raise his hat again. Finally John Rex got over there and flushed the birds and they won the championship," said Freddie Rayl.

John Rex Gates recounted a humorous story on Joe. "He was scouting for Fred Arant and Fred couldn't run for some reason, and I ran Fred's dog for him at the trial. Everyone was talking about the rattlesnakes there. Joe had got more than a little boogerish about those rattlesnakes. The other scouts recognized this and started in on him, telling him that the rattlesnakes were going to jump up and bite him on the leg while he was riding his horse. I ran into Joe in the woods as we were both looking for our dog. I looked over at Joe and he didn't have his feet in his stirrups, he had his feet way up in the saddle like a jockey. I said 'Joe, what you doing, bud?' He said, 'I'm scared of these rattlesnakes, Mr. Gates.' "

Almost forgotten is that Joe was quite a harmonica player. He liked to sit around and play the harmonica and sing songs about dogs. Freddie Epp remembers Joe singing a song for him about Black Belt and how great he was. He also stated that Joe was always straight, would help you find your dog, and would always tell you where your dog was.

These scouts, and many more men and women like them, have contributed more to the sport of field trialing that are often given credit. In the future, it is hoped that another scout will be elected to the Field Trial Hall of Fame to join Ben (Man) Rand.

David Johnson, 2021
Courtesy of David Johnson

Ben Rand, Saturn, Paladin, Luminary, and Ben "Man" Rand
Photo courtesy Billy Morton

Ben "Man" Rand force breaking Allure
Photo courtesy Billy Morton

Loren "Peck" Kelly with Satilla Wahoo Pete
Photo courtesy of The American Field

Joe Bush with Fiddler's Pride at the National Breakaway

Photo courtesy of Joe Bush

The Southwestern 1958–1977

The Best of Times

To know where we are in the field trail game we must, from time to time, pause to look back at where we have been. The past performances of truly great dogs beg not to be forgotten. Precious memories of handlers, scouts, and lovers of the game become more distant with each passing season and need to be preserved for those who will pick up the torch in the future. In the late fifties and sixties, Bill Allen, James Cottingham, Dave Fletcher, Hal Davis, and Chuck Hodges, among others, covered the running for the American Field. A deliberate effort has been made to include many of these eloquent and wonderfully descriptive examples of penmanship in reporting the Southwestern, its personalities, and dogs. If a place can be loved, then it is the hallowed grounds of the old Southwestern. It had an almost magical effect on those who rode through the tree-lined pastures or experienced the cool November wind against their face while riding alongside

Henscratch Mountain. Although the Southwestern had been run several years before 1958, this author has chosen 1958 as a starting date in order to include available firsthand accounts.

In its heyday, the Southwestern was the finest venue to run and view a big running dog other than the prairies of the Dakota's and Canada. Bill Allen praised the area in the Field, saying, "Without reservation, it must be pointed out here that no other state, so far as this writer knows, has done as much for field trials within its boundaries as Arkansas. The Fletcher Creek Refuge is a monument to all the men who have worked on it, especially to Ben Hogan, and Gene Bush and Robert Parker of the commission staff and the biologists and rangers who have improved and protected it. This writer's annual praise for these grounds is not unfounded. The area is a measuring stick by which all field trial venues, except those reserved to prove certain things and to single out certain types of dogs, can be gauged."

In 1958, Marshall Loftin had a firsthand account of the running as well as learning a valuable lesson from John Gates, who handled Storm Trooper. "John would get me to ride front for him and would always qualify more than one dog in the two- hour finals. I'd ride the front in case John got off looking for his dog, and if it came to the front I'd take him. My scout would take an extra horse for Peck to ride, as Peck rode hard. That country was big and the dogs would run wide. We were in the first brace after dinner and John was running LeBaron, who was braced with Tiny Wahoo. Tiny Wahoo was a good dog. On the first brace you would go straight up over Henscratch Mountain and get into the valley on the other side, make a big loop and then come back down the mountain in another place. When you got back over the mountain, you were on real good prairie country where you could see real good. John turned loose LaBaron, who was a good dog, but he didn't do nothing that day. Tiny Wahoo hunted for a while, ran off, and was counted out. John Gates was still running LaBaron and wasn't doing nothing. John just kept riding and blowing his whistle, just like he was winning the field trail. And I thought to myself—I was young—why doesn't he pick him up? We had Storm Trooper in the next brace. He just kept running him. He went all the way and made the loop in the mountain and in tight country just like he was winning the trial. When he got over the mountain into the prairie country, he turned to the judge and said, 'Well, I believe I will pick him up.' Later he told me, 'I wasn't going to turn Storm Trooper a loose up there on in that tight country where he might go and point a bird where we couldn't find him. I wanted him in this open country where we could win it.' We put Storm Trooper down on that prairie and he put on a show if there had ever been a show. He won it and I believe he had seven or eight finds. He knew what he was doing and wanted to get that bad course behind him and use the good course with Storm Trooper running." In 2013, Bill Allen added, "Storm Trooper, 'Dan' as he was called, was the most unappreciated pointer I ever watched . . . a very brainy dog with unexhaustable bottom."

The 1959 rendition featured a royal entry including Hattie of Arkansas, Susan Peters, Home Again Hattie, Medallion, The Arkansas Ranger, Safari, and Paladin's Royal Heir. Bill Allen reported, "Gendarme was head and shoulders and aloft tail above his competitors in the finals. He, The Arkansas Ranger, and Wonsup were the real stars of the qualifying series. For all intents and purposes, as this reporter saw it, Gendarme was picked up on point after two hours of solid bird hunting. We saw seventeen coveys in the two hours—including those ridden up—almost as many as seen in some whole days. With six perfect finds and a beautiful downwind stop to flush out a covey, the powerful, bottomless 'Pepper' dog eclipsed thirty other bird dog greats and nine other championship contenders in the two hour finals of this stellar event. The final ten with their bracings were Drucie of Arkansas with Chuckaluck, Paris with the Tennessee Ranger, Gendarme with the Arkansas Ranger, Honest Injun with Woody of Arkansas, and the Roving Ambassador with Wonsup." Bill Allen later remembered Gendarme and the running. "Under the whistle of Spot Suttle, this was my most memorable performance of a dog at the Southwestern."

"The Tennessee Ranger,"—as reported by Bill Allen—"brilliant young white and liver pointer dog, owned by L. V. Sevier III and handled by John S. Gates, was named the winner upon completion of the 1960 rendition's final heat. 'Tex,' as he is known in the field, found game three times perfectly and stood stanch while his bracemate chased birds in front of him to win the nod from judges W. A. Dumas of El Dorado, Arkansas, Henry Davis of Magnolia Springs, Alabama, and W. I. Brandon of Carbondale, Illinois."

Perry Milkles, of Booneville, remembered that "John S. Gates dogs could really run and stretch out. The old Southwestern was a place where a running dog could really be shown and you could really see the dogs. He had the runningest dogs in the business and was a true southern gentleman. He would always come with one of the best scouts in the business, Peck Kelly."

Bill Allen reporting for the Field in 1961, saying, "The Arkansas Association and this reporter have been unabashedly carrying on a love affair insofar as field trials are concerned for several years in this magazine. For whatever shortcomings there may be for some to travel to Booneville, the open stakes held over the Fletcher Creek quail refuge are worthy of any fancier's praise. All of the owners who made the trip this year and many who attended the National Amateur Quail Championships here a decade ago have praised unstintingly the attractive expanse of grounds. But never before this year have there been so many quail. This is due, in great measure, to Bob Parker, resident quail refuge worker. Every quail on the refuge in the shadow of Henscratch Mountain is as much cared for and as jealously guarded as though it were Parker's child."

Allen continues, "Polaris Pete, hard-running white and liver pointer dog owned by Dr. H. H. Vaughan and J. B. Brasswell Jr. and handled by John Gates, came through in the two-hour finals to gain the crown by virtue of a slashing, joyously, indomitable race with six finds, one of them etched ineffaceably in memory. Pete worked through almost impenetrable briars to point a bevy solidly on the banks of a swollen creek, a place where Lee had trouble flushing, but Pete's propensity for digging in was bore out. Pete knows that bevies may be near watercourses, for he pointed this one almost belly deep in water. In the tough two-hour test, Pete proved to be sound of wind and limb and his hard-driving quest, combined with a dandy game tally, carried him to the title.

"Safari, distinguished white and orange pointer bitch, owned by Sellers Vredenburgh and handled by John Gates, won the 1962 renewal," reports Bill Allen. "She rendered a glittering two hours highlighted by two solid bevy finds, and each quail discovery was well earned in the finals. She finished in a veritable burst of power and glory to capture her fifth championship crown. This was the 61st Championship for handler John Gates." Perry Mikles remembered going into John Rex Gate's room in this general time frame with Oklahoma Flush laying on one bed and Safari laying on the other.

Handler John Rex Gates won the 1963 edition with Polaris Pete owned by Dr. Herbert Vaughan. Bill Allen reported, "Pete had two excellent finds and two unproductive points, and he had a strong finish. Reflecting the paucity of game this year on this celebrated venue and the lack of completely clean performance by eight admittedly great dogs, no runner-up was named. It should be said here that Polaris Pete has always been something of a firebrand on these widely sung grounds. It is remembered that Pete was runner-up in 1960 and captured the title in 1961." This year, (1963) cover was short enough so that a Willie Hoppe might have had several billiard runs on the ground anywhere on the courses. Birds jumped from in front of dogs, tantalized dogs, young and old, and ran away from dogs as any old bird hunter can tell you they will do in light cover when they are aware of what V. E. Humphries calls 'a big pumpkin-eyed pointer breathin' down their gullet.' "

A very descriptive account of winning the 1963 Southwestern was offered by John Rex Gates. The account also is a tribute to the knowledge and craftiness of Leon Covington. "On that day my dad was running Pete. Dad had always told me to never give up on a dog. Pete had a couple of unproductives. I told my dad to not give up on him and to let me finish running him. He then said, 'Come here, Bull, and you run him.' I started to handle him and he had a couple of finds in the last twenty minutes. Pete qualified. We got him qualified and I told my dad that what he said was true. After the qualifying something happened and Dad had to go back home, that's why he did not ride front for me. I guess I was about twenty-one years old when I won the Southwestern in 1963. When I went out there, I didn't know much about the country. As a handler, you really need to know the courses. My dad gave me this advice when I was thinking about the course and what I was going to do: 'Bull, I'm going to tell you what I want you to do. I want you to hire Leon Covington, one of the smartest dog men that ever lived to ride front for you. Cov knows all the courses, he knows everything out there. He knows all the hooks and crooks to get around the courses. Tell him what you will do for him if you win the championship.' I told Cov if you ride the course for me and keep my dog on the course, I'm going to share the purse with you. Cov was a very smart guy. I had come up under my daddy and I had known him since I was a little bitty boy. My dad also told me to hire Roger, Cov's scout. Roger, like Cov, knew every foot of that country. If you get out there and start winning the trial, listen to Cov and you will be guided right. Pete was running for the championship as he was called back. We had a couple of finds and then a find about five minutes before pick up time. After that we headed toward the gallery to get the dog headed back to the front. Cov ran up to me and said, 'Boy, I want you to listen to me now. We got to work this thing to when you get back, Pete will win.' Cov then asked, 'When you hit this dog with a whistle, will he run to the front?' And I said yes he will. Cov then replied, 'I want you to go to the front until about a minute and a half to go.' He paused and then asked, 'Can you make that dog heel?' I said, 'Yes, sir, I can make him heel pretty good.' Covington then said with thought, 'Now take it easy, because we don't want to hit the front until we have about three minutes left.' We came to a gate and he told Roger to get down and fumble around with it for about a minute and be sure not to get it open too soon. So Roger played like the gate was hung up; when the gate was finally opened, Cov said, 'You have about a minute before you will be in front of the gallery with about forty-five seconds left. You got it won and we don't want to lose that dog. We want to come out just to the base of Henscratch Mountain. When you have about a minute to go, I want you to hit him with that whistle and I want him to be headed up the edge of that hill when they say to pick them up. We've got the trial won, but we will put the icing on the cake in this last minute.' Cov was an artist with a dog. He could out think and out do most folks, that's why he won so many field trials." Pete won the trial with this superb performance.

"Pete was a good, honest bird dog," recalled Gates. "He ran to hunt and would go just as far as he needed to. He was persistent and had a natural instinct bred into him that man can't put into a dog. He wanted to stay in front, but you could rely on him to check back with you. Pete had a lot of natural ability and he was a very powerful bird dog. He hunted ninety percent of the time in a trial, ran to hunt, was very consistent as to showing up right and lived to find birds."

"The Southwestern was known as one of the toughest trials to win because you had to qualify your dog in one-hour heats and then the judges had the option to call you back for a two-hour heat," commented Marshall Loftin. "I've heard John Gates say the trial at the Southwestern was extremely hard on a dog because it was big country and was as hard on a dog, the two hours, as three hours was later in the year."

Andy Daughtery was another young handler who used the camaraderie of the Southwestern as a learning experience. "I would sit and listen to 'Cov' and Fred Arant and try to learn. I loved to talk to Fred Arant because he raised dogs and he was an outstanding dog man. Fred told me this advice about puppies. The first thing he saw that he did not like he got rid of the puppy."

Handled by Stub Poynor and owned by W. E. Martindale, Checkmate Swaps claimed the 1964 title. James Cottingham reported, "Swaps, white and liver pointer, had one excellent find and raced strongly throughout, with well-directed casts." In the finals, "Swaps pointed with Poynor working hard to raise birds but couldn't do so, so Swaps had a chance for relocation which he handled quite well. He moved up a ditch and came to point while, standing in water but he was never more stylish than right here. At this time birds were raised."

"History repeats itself!" Hal Davis reported. "Checkmate Swaps returned to Booneville and repeated his 1964 win for owner W. E. Marindale and handler Stub Poynor. Conditions were severe. After a five-week drought, the heat broke all-time records for this time of year. Checkmate Swaps stood out like a statue over the field with the best bird work, the finest race and the greatest endurance. Swaps' finish was one of the best in some of the hottest weather in the history of November records in Arkansas, and he ran in a wind that ranged from twenty to forty miles per hour. Swaps three finds came as a result of him hunting them up in dense thickets and cover."

A regular at the Southwestern was Mary Oliver from Little Rock. She loved field trialing and would tell things just as they were, whether someone wanted to hear it or not. Hoyle Eaton remembered, saying. "Mary Oliver was a character. She spoke just what she thought and she didn't pull any punches. They had a puppy stakes there and she had brought some puppies to run. John Gates had also brought some bigger puppies to run and she asked him, 'Mr. Gates, how did you get your puppies so big so fast!' Most field trailers will understand the meaning of her remark.

Bill Allen remembered her in this manner, saying. "Mary Oliver was a very knowledgeable, very opinionated, very loyal dog fancier. She had some really great dogs, none of whom were ever the less for having had her as owner. She usually knew what she was talking about because she rode a lot. She, like all kennel-eyed-fanciers, was at her best when she took her handlers' words as gospel over that of everyone else. Even the great Jack Harper got misquoted sometimes. Mary really, genuinely loved field trials and pointers obsessively."

According to Marshall Loftin, "Mary Oliver was very instrumental in the trial. She bred and raised her own dogs and they were hard to beat. When her dogs were ready to campaign, she would place them with Jack Harper. She would also handle her dogs in amateur stakes and won a lot of them." National champions Home Again Hattie, and The Arkansas Ranger were both owned by Mrs. Oliver. Perry Mikles recounted, "Mary had an old high-stepping walking horse, and when I was fourteen or fifteen years old she would hire me to ride the horse until about noon and take the spunk out of it and then she would ride it." It was a sad note in 1975, while attending the Southwestern, her house in Little Rock was ransacked and all of her field trial trophies were stolen, which the Field reported as "a deep, irreplaceable loss."

Bruce Harris reported in 1966 that, "John Hogan Boy, white and orange pointer dog, just past five years of age, owned by A.J. Knight and handled by Ernest Allen, won the Southwestern Championship, feature event of the mammoth Arkansas Field Trial Association's program at Booneville, Arkansas. John Hogan boy, or 'Joe,' qualified for the two-hour finals when he ran in the eleventh brace of the series. He delivered a wide slashing race with his first find coming at fifteen minutes far ahead and right on woods line. His location and manners were beyond reproach. The second find came at fifty minutes, again far and ahead on the course. There was no question that he was the top qualifier." During his two-hour championship, Harris reports, "Joe ran an inspired forward ground race and scored four spectacular finds."

Recounting the Southwestern, Marshall Loftin remembered, "Just an ordinary dog could not win there. Red Water Rex was a strong competitor out there, he was tough. A Storm Trooper put in a strong performance for John Gates. Warhoop Jake won it and was one of the great dogs. Warhoop Jake was a strong bird finder, would run real big, and could just find and point more birds than the other dogs. There was something about the Mississippi River that when you took dogs who had been trained or were running east of the Mississippi River and went west with them it was hard to win with them. When you took dogs west of the Mississippi River and came back east, the same thing held true. Swaps was trained in Marion, Oklahoma. Stub didn't go to a lot of trials, especially in Georgia and Alabama. Leon Covington lived on the edge of the trial grounds and trained quite a bit there. One thing about Leon Covington is that he never tried to go to the so called easy trials, he went to the tough ones where winning really meant something."

David Fletcher reports in a beautifully descriptive fashion the 1967 running including a plea to the state of Arkansas to keep the grounds available for field trials. In the Field, it was reported, "White Knight's Bullet, youthful white and orange pointer dog, who won't celebrate his fourth birthday until March, utterly surpassed a classy field of forty to win the Southwestern. Bullet is registered to the ownership of Maness Barlett, and was handled by Dexter Holye Eaton. He claimed his callback in the two-hour finals with a fine hunting effort and a single immaculate find. The performance of White Knight's Bullett in the initial series was not an hour what one could describe as showy, for Bullett dug into the wooded places and had several absences. The pattern was surging, and the single find left no doubt that this dog had utterly scoured the country. His find was in the thickest brier and sedge corner of the grounds and it took grit and determination to simply get to the point of contact. In the two-hour finals, Bullett ran perhaps a stronger race than his original hour. The course was more open in several places and he loomed largely ahead. He was looking for birds and finding them. He handled the six chances without a bobble and added a back of his bracemate. His final bevy put the icing on the cake, as it was the result of a particularly intelligent and huge forward cast. Bullett had a great finish." Hoyle Eaton clearly remembered the finals, saying, "It was so foggy you could not see your dog. I had no idea they would have you turn your dog loose in that kind of fog but they did. We just happened to ride up on him as he was pointed out there in one of those big pastures. That happened one more time and then the fog started rising and we could see some then. Later he was on point where Mary Oliver and Maness Barlett could see him near the blacktop. They were hollering and carrying on but nobody heard and not long after the birds left and he took out toward me and had a heck of a race."

A forerunner of things to come was reported, "The fly in the ointment currently seems to be the fact that the tuberculosis disease has been conquered by modern science, and little need is held for the Sanatorium, which was formerly required for cattle pasture in connection with purification of milk for the institution. It is currently a political issue to dispose of the grounds to private bidders as a tax ease on the community. Sad will be the day when western Arkansas can no longer show the field trial fraternity its legacy of prime quail country in which to run a high-stepping bird dog."

"Aging, yet seemingly indestructible Red Water Rex, seven-year-old white and liver pointer dog, added his fifth title by topping ten second series contenders," David Fletcher reported in 1968. "Jointly owned by E. B. Alexander and W. T. Pruitt and handled by Dexter Hoyle Eaton, he appeared in the very first brace of the two-hour final, and scored on four bevies." In the two-hour finals, Fletcher adds, "To be sure, Rex was not in his finest running form the initial hour of the final series. He hunted with sage knowledge of where to find quail but his footwork was not overly inspiring. Rex began with a stylish point on a beautiful cast, but only a domestic chicken resulted. Rex added an unproductive in open pasture then, at the hour, scored perfectly on a bevy along an interesting hedge line. From this time on, Rex had a bracemate, and he picked up his enthusiasm greatly. The dog made some huge casts to the ninety-minute mark, utter brilliance in his work, and he was flying to his task. In heavy corridor the final thirty minutes, the chill of late afternoon crept in and birds began to move, with the air seemingly losing its dryness. Scenting appeared improved. Rex was tired, he had fought the punishing briers, delved without quarter into the heavy regions, and it was only his great heart that kept him going. He handled a bevy acceptably, in the trail, then added two more the final five minutes within curse corridor through heavy woods." Hoyle Eaton commented that "Red Water Rex looked like hamburger after running through the briars in winning the championship. Going back to the clubhouse with him after the brace, he still had some bottom left and wanted to go hunting."

Fletcher reported, "Cattle have been removed in great numbers and cover has thickened. Not to be vindictive, but briers and sapling growth are encroaching, feed plots need tending, and brush clearing would be a blessing in places."

Andy Daughtery remembered going to Booneville as a young man, saying, "I loved the grounds, and at that time there were plenty of birds. The first year I went, Red Water Rex won the championship. It was a big trial then. They had big bottoms and long grass areas, and it was a great place to run dogs."

Professional trainer Leon Covington lived on the edge of the trial grounds for several years. All who knew him acknowledged that he was one of the field trial game's great characters. Marshall Loftin remembers two instances of Cov living up to this billing. "Cov was running a dog named Echo, it pointed, he held his hand up, and didn't nobody answer it, although all of them saw him. Cov could sometimes have a short temper, so when they didn't answer again, he turned around and said, 'Hell, I said point, judges.' Right when he shouted, ole Echo jumped right in the middle of the birds and they were flying right at Leon with Echo chasing them like a puppy, barking at the birds. Everybody got a big laugh out of it except Cov. Another year, Eco had pointed birds in some little bushes. He jumped around and flushed the birds, caught one, and brought it to Cov."

Bill Allen remembered and shared this humorous story involving Cov. "Once, my wife Betts flew out and I picked her up in Fort Smith. That night, after Marshall Lortin and Bob Lee had left our room and Cov remained for 'just one more' . . . Betts finally decided to send a message. She went into the bathroom, stayed a while, and came out looking like Marcel Marceau in a fright wig. 'Wha's SHE a-doin?' Cov barked. 'She's gettin' ready for bed,' I laughed. 'It's late . . . why don't she go to her OWN room to get ready?' Cov pleaded. 'This is her room . . . our room . . . ' I laughed. 'Well, dayum,' Cov said in falsetto, 'I been WONDERIN' why y'all didden go to your room!!!' "

The 1969 rendition saw Red Water Rex capture his second Southwestern title. Bill Allen reported, "Red Water Rex, birdwise and fleet of foot, won the Southwestern Championship with two well-handled covey finds in this two-hour finals heat. The championship did not feature a lot of bird work, but Red Water Rex added to his laurels in a brilliant performance when the other entries failed to find more than one covey in the championship series. Allen also reported that "The grounds are not protected as they once were from poachers, and with the cattle operations ended there are no riders to scare away these two-legged predators. It was reported that one man, living here on the grounds, boasted to a group in Booneville that he had killed four hundred or more birds on the grounds."

"Red Water Rex, nine-year-old quailmaster,"—as described by Bill Allen in 1970—"claimed complete domination over the grounds of the Arkansas Field Trial Association and retired the O. C. Bailey trophy with his third straight win of the Southwestern Championship for trainer Hoyle Eaton. It was the glamorous pointer's ninth title! Rex had three brilliant finds in his final two hours and his finest final half-hour in more than a year, even eclipsing his finish here last year. This year, quail were scarce and grounds were rough and even impassable in places. Rex overcame all obstacles." Allen would later write, "This was Red Water Rex's best ever showing (except maybe the Continental)."

"I always thought I did better in endurance trials because of the hour qualifying and the two-hour finals," Hole Eaton remembered and shared. "The trial started around the eleventh of November and it was hot with lots of briars. It was rough. My dogs could handle the rough stuff better than others. A dog could distinguish himself there quick."

"As far as intelligence in a bird dog, Red Water Rex and Oklahoma Flush were two of the greatest pure ole dee bird dogs that ever walked," Perry Mikles recalled. "And they were super, super, super smart. A bird dog what was hunting and not just running on those old grounds could look like a million dollars because they ran on four thousand acres and you did not come close to crossing the same place twice. They were super great bird dogs. I have noticed this throughout the years with several great dogs: Riggins White Knight, Red Water Rex, Oklahoma Flush, Safari, that ole bitch of Andy Doughtery's, and Barshoe Buzzsaw. Tommy Davis's dogs always exhibited this. They were all great bird dogs but had one thing in common, they all had camaraderie and a connection to their handler. They finished those dogs back in those days because those dogs wanted to finish. The camaraderie between those dogs and those handlers John S. Gates, Hole Eaton, John Rex Gates, Leon Coventon with Lone Survivor, and Andy Doughtery were unmatched. It was not uncommon for the dogs to sleep in the rooms with them and be hauled around in the cab of the pickup. They were truly companions to those handlers."

In 1971, as reported by Chuck Hodges, "Ormond Smart Alec, scintillating six-year-old white and liver pointer dog, owned by Frank Matthew III captured his third title by winning the prestigious Southwestern championship. Alec, handled by D. Hoyle Eaton, qualified with a huge race and one find, and ran his thrilling two hours with two dug-out quail finds." For the first time the Arkansas Game and Fish Commission supplanted the native quail population with nine-hundred quail released two months before the trial."

Another bit of fun among the brethren at Booneville involved "Man" Rand as told by Marshall Loftin. "When Billy Morton started to run, he had a top-notch scout who is now in the Hall of Fame, Man Rand. We were running right down the side of Henscratch Mountain, knowing that most likely the birds would be on the side of the hill. Well, some of us dog trainers that didn't have nothing to do but stir up something decided to play a trick on Man Rand. We thought that the dog he was scouting would go to the hillside and point birds, so we got Man aside. We told Man, 'You had better watch going up on the hillside because there are coyotes and wolves up there. And they will wait until you ride by on your horse and they will knock you off your horse and get on top of you, and you better be careful if you go up there hunting a dog.' Billy turned his bitch loose and it wasn't any time that she went up on the hillside, and he asked Man to go up there looking. Man wouldn't go and rather went behind a bush, thinking he could not be seen. Me, Bud Daughtery, and others just died laughing. Man was not going to go on the hill. About the third time she went up there, she must have pointed some birds, was lost, and didn't finish because Man would not go upon the hill."

Bill Allen reported in 1972, "With all the heart and power one could want from a dog, Texas Allegheny Mike, five-year-old white and orange pointer dog, won the Southwestern with a performance like those of the glorious sixties, with five coveys and a single and a gritty, forward, powerful and growing race under frigid conditions." Owned by Louis Wilson and Dr. R. C. L. Robertson and handled by Guy Smith, "It is the proof of every word he (Smith) has ever spoken about Mike. Always the stylish and the supreme bird finder, Mike was fit to show his wares for 120 minutes. He loved every minute of it, got stronger as the shadows lengthened and the ground water got chiller. He began hunting straightaway and found his first covey in the woods on the Henscratch slopes, acorn feeding, and although they walked all around him and flushed under him, Mike just flinched higher and loftier. The brace ended at the clubhouse and everyone knew the result."

The great female pointer, Monte Bello Peggy, won in 1973. Chuck Hodges reported that the "Smart and sparkling five-year-old white and liver pointer bitch, owned by Herbert and Libby Courtney and handled by Marshall Loftin, fresh from winning runner-up awards in the hard-fought Oklahoma Open Championship, made the short hop down to Booneville, Ark., and with an outstanding ninety-minute performance, punctuated with three crisp 'dug-up' covey finds, vanquished the talented field of thirty-one pointers and three setters. Having witnessed her performance in this titular event and that of the previous week at Inola, in this reporters opinion, Peggy was indeed sharp in her ground work here, but she was even sharper in Oklahoma, and this being said with no intention of taking anything from the championship performance here for it was of championship quality all the way." This was the first year that the Southwestern featured ninety-minute heats and not the hour qualifying and two hour finals.

When asked about bitches winning the Southwestern Perry, Mikles replied, "There has been quite a few pointer females that have won the Southland and the old Southwestern. I think as a whole the female is basically smarter, not as hard-headed and more intense on what they are doing rather than just running. If a dog could run an edge, which the Southwestern had a great amount of, they could look like a million dollars. It was nothing to see those old bitches that were great bird dogs; they wouldn't be what you classify as great prairie dogs, but you put them on that edge and they would run that edge as far as the edge would go. Because of this, they instantly became great big running dogs and because of their intelligence and the fact that the birds would often be on the edges, this made them hard to beat."

History repeated itself in 1974 as Monte Bello Peggy again won the coveted title. Chuck Hodges reported, "Monte Bello Peggy, scintillating white and liver pointer female, coming six years of age, has been the ballerina prima donna of the all-age major circuit since the beginning of the season. In four titular outings, this sizzling, animated sprite has captured three big crowns, and in winning the 22nd running of the prestigious Southwestern championship at Booneville, Ark, for the second year in a row, let it be known she enjoys the limelight and aims to please her audiences. Peggy seems to run as if airborne. She strikes the ground lightly and travels with all the class a connoisseur could ask. Her rapport with Loftin is something else!

They seem tuned to each other and give the appearance that she would thread a needle if called to do it."

"Peggy was a real good hedge running dog and the Booneville grounds fit her," Loftin recalled. "Peggy and I were always on the same page together. She was so smart, if she did something wrong in training and you corrected her, she never did it again. She had heart, endurance, and guts."

"Buckboard," Chuck Hodges reported in 1975, "puissant three-year-old white and liver pointer male, burned this wide-open course in a blistering and intelligent effort and scored one of those limber-like, dug up covey finds and a back to capture his second career title. Owned by Dr. Dorwin Hawthorne, handled by Bud Daugherty, and scouted by Andy Daugherty, ran his effort in the dry, hot conditions that obtained and finished his route on a way-out intelligent cast released at a breakaway. Buckboard ran his winning effort in the fifteenth brace, the first of Monday afternoon when the thermometer stood in the high 70s and only a whisper of a southerly breeze was blowing to cool things under the bright sun." Even with the high temperatures, Hodges reported Buckboard was " . . . digging in and popping smartly to a flying finish."

Chuck Goodall reported in 1976 "Miller's White Cloud, illustrious son of an illustrious sire, proved again by the umpteenth time that class will tell by winning the twenty-fourth renewal of the Southwestern championship. 'Mike's' performance under the educated whistle of D. Hoyle Eaton in the ninety-minute series against a field of twenty-one other fine bird dog contenders, was outstanding in race, bird finding, and response to command. It was apparent, as he sped down the distant timber line, when time was called that his race was superior and that he was the dog to beat."

"Miller's White Cloud was a heck of a dog," recounted Hoyle Eaton. "Some days he didn't have bird hunting on his mind and just ran, but if he had bird hunting on his mind, he was hard to beat."

"Rex's Cherokee Jake," as reported by Linda Hunt in 1977. "Larry Mitchell's pointer, wins title, and Smarty Gal is runner-up. Rex's Cherokee Jake, white and liver pointer male, captured his third title in tandem here on the grounds. Jake had scored one impeccable find in his ninety-minute heat." In remembering Rex's Cherokee, Hoyle Eaton said, "He was a sensational derby and he won the derby of the year. Sometimes on the breakaway, he could get bug-eyed and run to big. He would run so far that he could not hear me and we would lose him. One day I was working him and we lost him and could not find him. On the fourth day after his disappearance, we were working some dogs and found him lying at the truck when we came back. He was really cut up and was a mess. After that incident, he went on the rest of the season and won five championships. I really think him getting lost for those four days make him think twice about getting out of range of my whistle."

In 1978 a meeting was held at Mary Oliver's home in Little Rock with these interested parties: Dick Dumas, Mary Oliver, Leon Cantwell, Bob Brown, John Seawright, and Charlie Jackson. John Seawright stated that "The meeting was very diplomatic and graciously done with the officers of the Southwestern in Booneville thanking the new keepers of the Southwestern to be run at Camp Robinson." Time had taken its toll on the officers and those most responsible for the herculean task of putting on the trial at Booneville. This, plus the grounds suffering under the care of the Arkansas Department of Correction, were the two main reasons the trial officials decided to call it quits. Gone were the well-maintained grounds of the Sanatorium and the youth of the officers. Gone forever is the call of "point" coming off Henscratch Mountain, and gone forever is a legendary irreplaceable venue for the field trial community.

New grounds at Booneville were acquired by the Arkansas Game and Fish commission in 1985. The grounds of the Southland

Championship are approximately ten miles from the grounds of the old Southwestern. When describing the new grounds at Booneville, Bill Stubblefield added these thoughts: "The Southland is a course that is laid out on long, tree lined big fields where a dog can get lost real easy. Unless you have a real good scout to keep the dog located and keep him to the front, you will have problems."

Today, the old Southwestern clubhouse still stubbornly stands as if shaking a weathered fist at old man time, providing a gathering place for the ghosts of the past and for those yet to come. If one listens close, faint whispers of those greats of old may still he heard reverently recounting the best of times, people, and dogs. Perhaps, on cool, sunny November days, Cov and his friends still ride this hallowed ground waiting to call point, searching for Devine glory in what many consider field trial heaven.

Four Great Dogs of John Rex Gates

Texas Fight, Texas Allegheny Pete, Oklahoma Flush, and Safari

While many articles have been penned, justifiably so, honoring these four great dogs of John Rex Gates, the purpose of this article is primarily to capture firsthand descriptions, stories, and memories of these dogs before they disappear. John Rex Gates was asked to pick four of his many superior dogs for this story. He did so very quickly and without pause. This article is dedicated to John Rex, his contribution to field trials, and his many legendary dogs.

One of the greatest prairie dogs ever scouted, handled, and judged was Texas Fight. Fifteen of his twenty-one placements were earned on the prairie. He joined his sire, The Texas Squire, in the Hall of Fame. The rest of his pedigree is royal, to say the least: Flush's Country Squire, Paladin's Royal Flush, Paladin's Royal Heir, Paladin, Ariel, Muscle Shoal's Jake, Riggins White Knight, The Arkansas Ranger, Warhoop Jake, John Proctor, and back to the famous Rip Rap. Fight produced thirty-nine winners with 167 placements from twenty-two different dams.

Linda Hunt may have placed the ultimate description on Texas Fight, who had the call name Sam. "He was a big ole Hee-Haw prairie dog." John Rex said that he "could run like the wind, be solid on point, and be extra hard to handle." David Johnson described him as a "two-horse dog. Even when he was a pup, he was always the same—he loved to point and came out running." Joe Walker recalled him as "a beautiful dog on point and he was a running, running dog." His breeder was Edwin Brown, who had raised him as a puppy. John Rex remembered his early training. "Tony Terrell was responsible for him past a few months old. He didn't go to any field trials, but Tony was a real good dog man. He worked him in Texas as a puppy in the spring of the year when Sam was a coming derby, and he did a great job with him. The way we used to do it, we had several different people raising puppies for us. In the spring of the year we would look at these puppies and pick out the ones we thought had the qualities we were looking for. We tried to look for the very best. They would then be carried north to Canada with us in the summer and be started off as derbies. The game department in Canada would let us start training on the fifteenth of July. My dad would always say, 'Son, if he is still doing what we want him to by the fifteenth of August, he will make it.' " Marshall Loftin remembered Sam as being broke, even as a derby.

Tommy Long was quoted in the American Field as saying, "John Rex told me that, so far as he knew, the dog had never made a mistake on game in a trial. I've heard other people talk about it, never seeing him do anything wrong around game. And he would scare you, he could relocate so fast. John Rex said he could win on that alone. Of course he had a mind of his own. He could do plenty of mischief. But it wasn't on game."

"He was just a great prairie dog," commented David Johnson, who remembered him well. "When you turned him loose, he would run as far as the eye could see. We were at Mortlach one year, out in that great big country, and the wind was blowing real hard right in his face. I really enjoyed watching him; the wind was blowing so hard his ears were flopping. He was really pointing those chickens and Hungarian partridges. All the talk at that trial was about his performance. He won the trial hands down."

John Rex Gates said, "Most of the Canadian championships back then had anywhere from fifty to a hundred entries. I don't remember exactly what year, but this trial was no exception. There weren't many birds being found and most of the dogs weren't pointing any birds at all. In an hour he produced eight or ten finds; he couldn't hardly run fifty yards across the prairie for pointing. We had eight finds and didn't win a nickel. He just went bird hunting that day instead of trialing like an all-age dog. I never once turned him loose without expecting him to run, but that day was an exception. He was usually hard to handle. If he would have run like he normally ran, all I would have needed was two finds to win. He was generally the type of dog that you didn't need to hide but rather to find."

"He was a great chicken dog," reminisced Linda Hunt. "When you turned him loose, it was like he had a flight pattern and that was to a bluff. He was the kind of dog who either won it big or not at all. Texas Fight was really a thrilling dog to watch. He looked good on point with plenty of style."

John Rex laughed while telling this story about Sam. "That dog had a mind of his own, no question about it. We had gravel in our kennels in Canada. Sam had the gravel plus a big rock in his. The rock was about as big as a football, was in his barrel, and he laid on the thing. There's no way it could have been comfortable as he would just lay on top of it. We thought we were doing the right thing and took the rock away from the kennel. Sam didn't sleep and barked and growled until we put the rock back in there; the boys started calling it his puppy. He adopted that rock as his own."

"In this part of the country," (the Southeast) stated Joe Bush, "he was hard to keep up with, but up there in Canada he was really good and hard to beat. I remember one time down here at the Masters Championship he was braced with Strong Man, who loved to fight. I was scouting Strong Man and Tommy Long had Texas Fight. We turned 'em loose and those jokers went out there right on the breakaway. Strong Man stopped to take a leak and it was on. Texas Fight ran over there by him; Strong Man grabbed him and slung him all over the place. After that it was the best I have ever seen Texas Fight handle. He went through there and had around seven finds and won the championship while Strong Man ran off. That was the only time I ever saw him handle in this part of the country. He handled like he was on a string that day." David Johnson added, "We finally got them separated and they picked up Strong Man shortly after. Well, Strong Man had Texas Fight so scared that he didn't run off, and he had a bunch of finds in that hour."

There is a strong argument to be made that Texas Fight was the best prairie and chicken dog of his generation and perhaps any generation. Those who saw him perform on the prairies still have very distinct memories of him.

Texas Allegheny Pete's story did not start with John Rex or with prepping to be an all-age competitor. His first trailing experience was with Dean Lord and shooting dog trials. "I bought the dog from Holland Chandler when he was about ten months old," recounted Dean Lord. "He was a big ole puppy and broke really easy. Back then we had a lot of birds. I bought him to be a bird dog and was going to make a hunting dog out of him. When he got older he got to running so big we couldn't handle him for bird hunting. He wasn't hard to handle, it was just he ran so big for bird hunting and the shooting dog circuit."

Mr. Lord continued, "I ran him when he was a derby in New York. That's where I met Bob Wehle. He rode up to me when I picked Pete up after having two finds. He said, 'Young man, they can run from now on and they will never beat him.' He had two solid broke finds in Baldwinsville, New York, that day. Pete was a very biddable dog who ran as big as needed. He was known for being a bird finder and for always being able to scrape up birds even when the other dogs were having trouble."

"He was as good a bird dog as I have ever seen in competition," Mr. Gates said with conviction. "Dean Lord called me and said that he had a dog that would make a great all-age dog. He could bring him down to shooting dog range but didn't want to because he was a natural all-age dog. He ended by saying, 'He will make you a hell of an all-age dog.' He was a real strong bird dog when I got him from Dean. The first time I saw him I was very impressed with him. My friend Dean Lord had that dog right. Dean is probably one of the smartest men with bird dogs there ever was. And that's a fact! All I had to do was go out there and turn him loose. I knew the first time I looked at him he was a great dog; I could see the bird dog in him. He ran to hunt birds."

"I got him when he was coming four," John Rex continued. "At age seven he developed a lung infection and died. If he had not died in his prime, he would have won several more championships. I won the Saskatchewan Championship with him—that stake probably had seventy-five to eighty of the best dogs in the world in it. He was called back in the second series. Marshall Loftin was one of the judges. They called Pete back with one of Howard Kirk's Gunsmoke dogs. Pete ended up being the winner. I think he had five finds."

A fact often overlooked when present-day discussions are held regarding Pete is that he had twenty-five or more shooting dog wins before competing with John Rex on the all-age circuit.

Hall of Famer Oklahoma Flush, call name Butch, "was one of the smartest dogs I ever trialed," John Rex proudly stated. "Butch showed this intelligence in the expressions on his face and in everything he did. He loved people and loved being the focus at a trial. Butch was the second dog in the history of the sport to win ten open championships. Back then, there weren't over ten to fifteen major championships in the world, and everybody ran in them. These trials would have fifty or more of the best dogs in the world ready to compete. I could walk with Butch if I wanted to bird hunt, or I could talk to him real easy and he would go out a hundred or two hundred yards and stay with you. You could hit him with a whistle while riding and let him know you wanted him to go, and he would go until he was as small as an aspirin tablet. If he didn't point, he would always come back and check with you. He would imprint you and your horse and could spot you at any time. Butch would cross in front of you three or four hundred yards, rare up, and pick your horse out. After that, all you would have to do is head your horse in the direction you wanted him to go and that's where he went. He had a built-in compass; some of these dogs don't have that and you can't put that compass in one unless he has a good start with it."

Marshall Loftin also remembered that it didn't matter where you turned him loose—he almost never got lost.

Oklahoma Flush was owned by Roger Keys, then after Keys's death, by Sellers H. Vredenburgh, who also owned Safari. K. L. Keesee raised him in Oklahoma. Sired by Paladin's Royal Flush and Baconrind's Sandy, who was a very fine bird dog in her own right, his pedigree was royal. In his pedigree are four national champions in the first two generations, Paladin, Ariel, Shore's Brownie Doone, and Sierra Joan. Three champions of the offspring of Baconrind's Sandy were in the same litter. Oklahoma Flush, Paladin's Royal Gold, and Royal Paladin Babe. During his career, he amassed twenty-four placements.

Hoyle Eaton remembered the first time he saw him. "It was Crab Orchard, Illinois, where the quail futurity was being held. He won it that year. He was a very consistent dog and strong, not the biggest running dog, but plenty big enough. He really would cover his country well and was a big, fine-looking dog."

David Johnson described him perfectly. "He was a big running dog but was the kind that would come back and look you up. He looked good on point, and when he pointed you didn't just hit out there in front of him, you had to get out a distance away and look for the birds. He had a strong, super nose and was an honest dog. Butch was a long, stocky-built dog, but when he hit the ground, he was an easy footing dog with a pretty stride and gait."

Joe Bush remembered him as "running like a locomotive."

John Rex recalled famed sports writer Jerome Robinson. "He asked if he was a good bird dog and if I could bird hunt over him. I told him, 'Yes, sir, he is a real good bird dog.' Mr. Robinson then said, 'You mean the dog that I saw run all over this county and run a mile out, you can bird hunt with him?' I said, 'Yes, sir.' Continuing, Mr. Robinson replied, 'Do you have a place in South Georgia we can work?' 'Sure,' I said, 'I got a place where we can move fifty or sixty coveys on a plantation.' 'Do you mind if I bring my brag dog with me and we turn these two dogs loose?' Mr. Robinson asked. So we went down, turned 'em loose, and walked. Butch hunted right in front of us like a bird dog should, and by the time we were through, I think the count was fourteen to one with Butch with the fourteen. He was then convinced that you could take a big running dog and bring him in to be a foot-hunting bird dog."

National Champion and Hall of Fame selection Safari was bred by Col. B. C. Goss at Mercer Mill Plantation out of Mercer Miller and Mercer Mill Judy and was owned by Sellers Vredenburgh. Prominent in her sire's pedigree is Fast Delivery and The Haberdasher. On the dam's side are The Texas Ranger and Tyson. Her early success came under the whistle of John S. Gates and later under John Rex Gates. It was reported in The Field that her winnings at the age of nine and one-half were $28,395, a huge sum for the time.

During her derby-year training, John Rex Gates recalled, "When we went to Canada we always made a list of our dogs and assigned each one a trainer, as you did not want one person working a dog today and another tomorrow. Burnt Rudolph was assigned to work Safari. After he had worked with her a good bit, my daddy asked him one day, 'Burnt, how is Judy doing?' Burnt said, 'Captain, she's a pretty good dog.' Burnt and Peck Kelley were out working with my dad one day. Peck told my daddy, 'Captain John, You had better look at ole Judy before the field trials start. She's a pretty good one.' I think he won the derby stake up in Canada that year with her."

"She was a consistent front-running dog and a very good bird dog," Hoyle Eaton remembered. "She was a good, good dog. The first time I was associated with John Gates was at Canton, Mississippi; we were training there. He was running Safari in a trial and I was riding, watching. She pointed by a fencerow and I was looking down to the lower end of it, and I saw a covey of birds fly. Nobody else saw them, so I made a comment to Bill Brown that I saw birds fly and she was credited with the find."

Mr. Eaton continued, "She had an orange-marked head and was a strong-looking female. While not straight up on point, she was plenty high and was a good-looking dog on point. One of her best qualities was that she was very biddable and wanted to please. They never had any trouble losing her because she was attached to her handler. She was not a super big running dog, but enough, and was prone to appear in just the right places. She would go bird hunting, but it was always to benefit her handler." These were traits that Marshall Loftin also remembered. John Rex remarked, "She was attached to my dad. When Dad couldn't handle any more, it took about six months for her to truly accept me and to do her best work."

"When she was a young dog, she really got to fooling with porcupines," Mr. Gates said. "Even after pulling a bunch of quills out of her, she just got worse and worse. Because of this, Burnt was getting after her pretty bad. It wasn't long that she started having unproductives on her game. We figured that was caused by us getting on to her too much because of her fondness for porcupines. We broke her off the unproductives in Georgia. When she would point, we would not even get off our horse to flush the bird. We would ride in front of her and flush the bird and kill it. You could do that in Georgia. That brought her out of it."

Mr. Gates continued, "Safari was just a very fine bird dog and a great running dog. She would run as big as the country allowed, was born with a built-in compass, and just wouldn't lose you in a trial. You could send her one way and then send your horse the other way, and sooner or later she will catch up with you. She was the first in the history of the bird dog world to win ten major all-age championships. I think her win in the Dominion gave her the tenth championship. Colvin Davis and I both were running dogs at this trial. Joe Hurdle and Paul J. Tredway were the judges. There was a second series at this trial in which Safari was called back along with The Hurricane. Both of these dogs were in the Gates string. We wanted the tenth championship really bad, but my daddy said very strongly we were not going to show any favoritism. Let the best dog win. There was a lot of pressure on Colvin that day as he was running The Hurricane against Judy."

Handlers on today's major circuit would love to have any one of these dogs much less four of their caliber. John Rex handled the best of the best with the skill and tenacity only other Hall of Famers can match.

John Rex Gates and Oklahoma Flush
Photo courtesy of The American Field

David Johnson and John Rex Gates
Photo courtesy of John Rex Gates

Three of the Best

A good shooting dog draped against brown grass in scattered, tall pines is a beautiful sight. They have to be snappy, run, and show extreme style while on point. There have been many successful shooting dog handlers, but only a handful can be deemed elite. Gordon Hazlewood, Shawn Kinkelaar, and Harold Ray fit into the elite category just like a tailor-made suit.

"I lived near Tomball, Texas, and started out as a bird hunter," Gordon Hazlewood remembered, his eyes gazing out a window, looking for times past. "I was laid off my job in November, ran an ad in the Houston paper regarding bird dog training, and was amazed that the calls just flooded me. After adding to my kennel, and in the process picking up a good number of dogs, I wanted to try a field trial. Back in the sixties, they had quite a few amateur field trials. It took me several tries, but I finally won a second place in an open shooting dog stake. Following that trial, there was a fellow who worked for the Duncan Coffee Company named Murry Pyland. He approached me about running his dog in a few shooting dog stakes. I started to look for trial-caliber dogs, and the first thing I knew, I got a few in my string. And after about three years, I began to get some I could win with. In 1969, I quit my job with Cameron Iron Works and after that, never looked back. It's been a full-time job for me since."

Harold Ray was raised on a dairy farm near the border of Maryland and Pennsylvania. His neighbor, Mr. Rodney King, commercially raised different breeds of bird dogs. "I had been in the hospital, and shortly after my release," Mr. Ray commented, "he asked me if I would like to go to an all-age field trial at Indian Town Gap. Mr. King was going to breed a dog to Magnum, who belonged to Dr. Alvin Nitchman. I watched the field trial and liked it. On the way home, Mr. King told me that some of the handlers would take boys to Canada and teach them about dogs. He took me back up there the next day and introduced me to Fred Bean. I visited with him, and he said to write him a letter when I got home. I did, but I had a skin infection that didn't look too good, so he didn't hire me and said that he had trouble in the past with some boys who had gone with him that he hadn't known long. They would get homesick and want to come home. He thought it would be best for me to start working for him in the fall, if I was still interested. Then, when it came time the next year, we would both have a better understanding of each other. So I wrote him a letter; I still have the original letter. His answer was on the back of it. That fall, I wrote him again and he said come on down. That's how I got started working for Fred Bean."

When he was eight or nine years old, Shawn Kinkelaar started hunting with his grandfather and uncle. "A few years into hunting in Illinois, birds really took a hit. I think an ice storm came through. About that time, my grandfather bought a real nice pup, which ended up being my first field trial dog. We went to our first field trial together. Our start was in walking trials, competing in NBHA trials where we made the national level. We ran puppies and derbies, which at that time you had to qualify on the local and state level just to go to the National. After high school, I started to get into the horse part of trialing—that is really a passion of mine, it always has been. We didn't have horses growing up for some reason, but I had friends that had them, and I loved riding. I pretty much knew that was what I wanted to do. After trying to go to college two or three times, I was always drawn back into dogs. I started working with several trainers, and it just got into my blood."

When discussing his mentors, Harold Ray relayed the following: "The fellow who I spent the most time and learned the most from was Bill Rayl. In a lot of ways, I was self-taught. Mr. Bean didn't go out with you, which kind of left you on your own. I read all the books on training I could get my hands on and listened to stories when trainers would get to talking up in Canada or at a hotel. Bill Rayl and I trained in Canada a lot. He was a sure 'nough dog trainer and taught me how to teach a dog to 'whoa.' You walk along with them, take a snap, and tap the dog under the chin when you go to get in front of them. After doing that a few times, the dog was naturally sitting down. So we had to take a pocketknife and tap them on the shin to make them stand up. When I got to Canada, the first year I got George Moreland's training ground in Manitoba, there were forty-three sections in it and only two cross fences. I had read in the American Field that Bill Rayl was in Big Bluff, Manitoba, so one Sunday afternoon, I went down and got to talking to him. He said he knew the grounds pretty well as he had worked some with George Moreland. So I asked him if he would mind coming up and kind of show me around the place. Bill came up and we got to working dogs together, and that went on for several years. I got to asking Bill about my problem: twelve dogs were in my string, and I had all twelve of them sitting down. I wanted to know how to get these dogs to stand up. He showed me what we later called the hitch—that's what Clyde Morton called it. There was an article Jerome Robinson penned in Sports Afield in 1972 with me using this hitch, putting the rope around the dog's waist and then Clyde sliding it through the dog's collar. I had hooks on trees that anchored the rope. If the dog followed you, then you could move him back into position. I got to using it and really thought I was a dog trainer. Years later, I asked Bill how he figured that out. He said that Clyde Morton had shown him. That's the way we learned things back then, through word of mouth or someone showing you. We didn't have books or the Internet. Two years later, I was judging the National Free-for-All. Mr. Billy Morton was there; we got to visiting and he invited me over. He asked me if Man had ever shown me the hitch, and I told him he had not. I went over to his house that night, and it was kind of like a kid in a candy store with all the A.G.E. Sage memorabilia, the old truck he would ship on the trains, Clyde Morton's bumper he would use on retrieves and his whistles. He got to showing me pictures on the wall and telling me when he went to work for Mr. Jimmy Hinton. He said that Man didn't use a rope, but a one-inch webbing. The picture on the wall was Man Rand working Allure with the hitch rope. The hitch was pretty instrumental in me getting dogs to stand up."

"I didn't, per se, have a mentor," said Gordon Hazlewood. "I had a lot of established trainers with dogs that helped me a lot. Steven Harwood, Dr. Joe Coleman, Dr. Fred Simmons, and Lester Shepherd. When I was about twenty or twenty-one, my parents built a house in Spring Branch, Texas, and there was a guy next door that had setters. That was before I ever thought about training dogs. He would carry me bird hunting, and you could walk out anywhere in that prairie country and find four or five coveys of birds in an afternoon. He was just a foot hunter but got me really interested in dogs and birds. After I got into training professionally, I got the chance to talk with some professional trainers. One of them, Dean Lord, really helped to set my standards. Over a period of twenty or thirty years, I watched his dogs, the way he handled them, and then added my own techniques to it. He is a super guy and one of the best handlers I have ever seen. I have never seen anybody get more from a dog than Dean. I tried to do things the way he did and conduct myself personally the way he did. Dean taught me to not put a bad dog on the ground but put a good one down. He said if you have an owner that has a dog that is just mediocre, you tell him that. If he is going to want to win, he will get a better one. I took his advice to heart, and that's what I tried to do. If my bottom dog was not good enough, I would go out and try and find a better one."

Shawn Kinkelaar credited his success to the fact that he got into training when he was young and had the opportunity to work with many different people. "I learned a little bit from everybody. It didn't hurt to start off at Gunsmoke Plantation with Herb Holmes, Billy Holmes, and Billy "Scope" Renfore. Jack Herriage, Butch Gerke, Bill Trabue, Harold Ray, Richie Robertson, Mike Wrenn, Marvin McDowell, Keith Martin, and many others took me under their wing and helped me out."

When asked which dog was his favorite to train or run, Mr. Kinkelaar couldn't separate several of the greats he has handled to championships. "I get asked this question almost on a daily basis. Here's what I will say today: Sunflower was the truest shooting dog that I have worked with or seen. Same range and same temperament, day in and day out. Swami was the most exciting field trial dog I have ever been around. She would make the hair on the back of your neck stand up. Hannabelle was pretty much on any category between Sunflower and Swami. She had strength, biddability, and excitement. Today, Thunderbolt falls right into that category."

Harold Ray was eager to answer which dog was his favorite to run. "It was Cash Master. When I started working shooting dogs, I had come off the all-age circuit. Running dogs were my favorite; they really had to run for me to be happy. Cash Master was one of those front-running dogs that could really run an all-age race but you never would lose him. He was lost one time in completion and that was in Green River, Illinois. They would run the qualifying before the championship. He had been gone for a little bit, so I sent my scout to the right to look for him. He didn't show and didn't show, and in a thirty-minute brace, you don't have a lot of time. So I decided to go off to the left. I knew he was on point; it was just a matter of where. We looked for him, along with the other handler, and still couldn't find him, so we didn't go any farther. They turned the next brace loose and there, about a hundred yards straight in front of us, was Cash Master, standing on point. It was the only time he was ever lost in competition. If you didn't holler, he would stop and wait until he could see you. I was told at one trial he came up to the clubhouse, got in the water trough and played, laid down on the ground and rolled and then would jump back in the water trough. About the time we came into sight, they said he took off across the road and pointed again. Wherever we went, he would have things figured out by the time we got to him on point. He maybe didn't have the best nose, but he had the best brain of any dog I ever ran."

Shawn Kinkelaar was not going to be painted into a corner when asked which dog was his favorite to run. "There is no way I would ever answer that question with just one dog. I'm going to go with two or three of them. What always comes to my mind was running Sunflower in the Invitational when she was coming on ten years of age. That was her second-to-last trial, and we had already planned her retirement. In the finals on the third day, at the thirty-minute mark, she had done everything but quit. She had no ground speed and was getting beat by her bracemate, a dog of George Tracy's. She had had two backs, and George's dog had two finds. When we topped the mountain at the thirty-minute mark at Camp Robinson, I didn't give her anything special and didn't do anything out of the ordinary, but somehow in her metabolism, something clicked, and she did as fine a performance in that final hour as any dog I have ever seen. Four finds, maybe five, and was running as hard at the finish as she was the first day. It was almost an act of God. My second-best race was when Thunderbolt had nine finds on wild birds at the All-American Championship three years ago. He set the record at that trial for the most finds. Just to handle that many birds was truly an exciting hour."

"High Tailed Reb was my favorite to run," Gordon Hazlewood responded. "I don't really know how he was bred; he was brought to me before DNA, and I'm not sure how old he was. After I started winning with him, everybody in the country claimed they had bred him. He had the most natural ability of any dog I ever ran. After the Cedar's Classic was over and Reb had won, a judge told me all the other trainers are scared to death of him. It didn't matter what country you turned him loose in, he made it his own training grounds. Unfortunately, he died young. Then I had a couple of females I won the National with. Texas Express Betty was a really nice dog, but you had to have really soft hands with her. I got her when she was three. She had a sister who was just the opposite. She won the National Amateur Shooting Dog Championship and about seven championships when it was all over and done. Betty also died very young. Another great one I had was Gerke Mayroll. I didn't get her until she was five. It took some convincing that she was not to retrieve a bird, but after I got her right, she won six championships. One of the best performances of a dog I really liked was Southland Mickey. He was a little dog. I remember when he won the Endurance down at Ardmore going away. He started out like a streak and finished that way. On his second or third find, his bracemate ran past him on point and flushed his birds. He then had the brace by himself. Sometimes that is a bad deal. If you have a dog that is getting a little tired, his bracemate will pick him up if he is competitive. He was just unbelievable at Conway in 2002 when he won the Invitational. He flew the whole three days. They called him a sprinter, and he was, but he would sprint for an hour and look for birds the whole time. He was a great little bird dog. His first trialing had been in Shoot to Retrieve, so I had to convince him to not break after the shot. These dogs would give it everything they had every time I put them on the ground. Back then, there would be seventy or eighty dogs in a championship, and I bet not over three of them would mess up. So in important trials, you had a bunch of dogs to beat, and that was very hard to do, especially if there were not many birds."

The best performance of a dog he handled was an easy question for Harold Ray. "I have two performances that really stand out. Cash Master's DD when she won the Futurity with three finds and a race just like Cash Master. She was perfection on the ground. Her bloodlines went back to Flaming Star. That performance was probably one of the best performances in the Futurity to this date. We were back that next spring in the championship. She drew the same course and pointed in almost the same tracks that she did in the Futurity and won the championship. The other performance was Flaming Star. He was running in a junior all-age stake up in Canada. The wind was really blowing. Flaming Star was running toward a rock pile, which had really no objectives, and several bare spots. Herman Smith called point for him. Flaming Star was pointing into the wind on bare ground; the flags on his tail were popping like a flag on a flagpole. I'll never forget that sight and him winning the trial. You could see him forever while going to the point. Another story I'd like to tell was a brace Flaming Star ran in the Georgia All-Age Championship. He was pointing bird after bird, and they called a second series. Dr. Nichman, who was very outspoken and a heck of a good dog trainer, told me this story. He was staying in the ole Anthony Wayne motel and sat down to eat with the judges. All they talked about was Flaming Star. He interrupted the judges' discussion. 'I want to ask you one question: how come Flaming Star didn't win?' They paused a moment and stated he was a little short, but he was a great dog and a great bird dog."

"The best performance of a dog I didn't handle goes to two dogs in one brace," Mr. Hazlewood was confident in his answer. "Harold Davis from Louisiana and Marshall Loftin were judging the Illinois Shooting Dog Championship one year. A second series was called. The trial was run in the spring of the year when the dogs were in their best condition. The judges ran these dogs almost three hours in the second series. It was just boom, boom, and boom. One dog would point and the other one back and then it would be reversed. I believe the dogs were Great Notion and Little Diamond. Eddie Rayl was running Little Diamond, who was a really great bitch; the male was Great Notion handled by Larry Moon. They ran those dogs three hours, and I rode up to Marshall and asked him if they didn't have a winner by now. They called pick up, and Great Notion won the trial. That was the best two dog performances I have ever seen."

When the question was posed to Shawn Kinkelaar, he said, "That's pretty easy. I helped Bill Trabue with Magdalene at the Illinois Championship. To start off with, I want to give credit to the judges, as the trial was run on pre-released pheasants. Bill was older at the time and would have never flushed those birds. As his scout, I blocked the birds with the horse before they could run off. That dog had nine finds and a solid hour. Every time we turned her loose, she would fade out of sight and we would find her pointed. It was absolute perfection. Anybody who saw Magdalene knows she was purely magnificent around her game. If it was not for the judges allowing me to block the birds, she would have had two non-productives on her first two finds."

"Twenty years ago there were so many trials held on wild birds; that's the main difference in trials and dogs today opposed to twenty years ago. When I first started," remembered Gordon Hazlewood, "you could go to Nixon, Texas, at a field trial and move twenty to thirty coveys a day. There were lots of wild birds in West Texas near Colorado City, Odessa, and Big Springs. The dogs that ran in those trials were a different kind of dog: they wild-bird hunted. Over the years, the trials have gradually dwindled down to where just a handful are run on wild birds. It takes a little different dog for the trials on wild birds. I'm not sure the dogs today are quite as good. We talked about that at a seminar I was invited to be on at Grand Junction a few years ago. One thing brought up, and agreed upon, was how many good dogs came out of being wild-bird hunted. I really think dogs are easier to train today. Twenty-five or thirty years ago, a dog was bred if they would run. The dogs today are so much better refined, mind-wise. A concern of mine relates to the future of trials; there are no young guys coming up. I'm afraid in ten years, on the west side of the Mississippi River, there will not be any professional field trailers. There may be a few amateur handlers, but who is going to train dogs for them? If you don't have pros, then you won't have amateurs."

"I don't consider it a difference in the dogs so much as a difference in the availability of birds and how you develop a dog today versus when I started," Mr. Ray thoughtfully responded, comparing today's dogs to dogs when he first started. "When I began, we were trialing on wild birds one hundred percent from Canada to Georgia. The difference is now we work dogs around a field or a bird box. In the past, dogs had to learn where birds lived. They had to look at the country, chose an objective, stay on the edge of a field, and chose the right side of the wind. All the dogs back then had to do these things. Now they have to follow a road and a path where birds were put down. That is the difference today.

"I remember watching John Gardner run a dog called Primrose Roudy at the All-American in Canada," continued Mr. Ray. "There were a lot of bluffs in that country. He would go to a bluff, catch the wind, go around the bluff and then go to the next one. He ran the whole hour and never went inside one. That was one of the prettiest prairie races I have ever seen. That's what really turns me on. Watching a dog think, go with you, be in front of you to the extreme and never take a wrong route. I really think the difference is the country and what the dogs are subjected to in training. I do feel we have dogs who are classier today, overall. There may be some improvement nose-wise, but I do remember the old dogs had pretty fine noses when I first started training for Mr. Smith. Certainly, a difference in training dogs is the electric collar. One rainy day, George Crangle, who had just retired, stopped by my kennel. The Bill Boatman electric collar had just come out. I asked Mr. Crangle what he thought about these new electric collars. He replied, 'There are two ways you break dogs: you wear out shoe leather and wear out horseshoes.' It was years later before I started using these collars. Over the years, I've learned which dogs to go on with and those not to waste your time on. That's where I am now. I've eliminated a lot of things I did in the past and tried to simplify my training process. When I break a dog now, I never use the word 'whoa.' I don't say anything; I let the dog go off body language. When I started this technique about ten years ago, I thought, this is the craziest thing I ever heard of. The first dog I broke like that was Classique's Boss, who Steve Hurdle ended up winning the National Shooting Dog Championship with the first year."

Shawn Kinkelaar believes the bloodlines we have today are more biddable and easily broken. "Back thirty years ago, unfortunately, there was a lot of heavy-handed training that had to be done, or you were not going to make those dogs work for you. As far as grounds go, I do not see a tremendous amount of difference between the grounds today and the grounds when I first started. I do think, however, twenty years ago we had more people putting an effort out into taking care of things. Having more people also includes having more money to go around and help. As far as competitiveness, the trials are still the same. The entry numbers are obviously not quite what they once were. I believe the dogs of today are better bred to go with you than they were back then. Judging-wise, I don't think there are quite as many to choose from, but for the most part, today's judges are good, honest people who like to see a good dog."

Gordon Hazlewood loved telling the story of an event that happened in Iona, Oklahoma. "Marvin McDowell was helping Jack Herriage run a dog. The wind was blowing and it was bad cold—I'm telling you probably in the teens. Marvin was holding a dog with his hand under the dog's collar with a brand-new, fifty-dollar pair of gloves he had bought. When the brace started, the dog took off before Marvin could get his hand out of the collar. He was hollering, 'Get him, stop him!' Jack didn't and just blew him to the front with his whistle. They never found the fifty-dollar glove."

Another remembrance from Mr. Hazlewood: "Frankie Ford was a retired dog trainer down in Texas, running a dog in Texas with me helping him. There were a few wild birds and rattlesnakes. Frankie called point as his dog was pointing up front about fifty or sixty yards. Art Crowell and Ronnie Crowell were judging. We started up there and Frank went to step off, and his foot hung in the strip on the off side over the horse. When that happened, the horse started running. I broke to the right to try and get in front of the horse, and the ground was bad covered in sand burrs. He got up when we got the horse stopped and said, 'Did you see the birds?' If he had one sand burr in his head, he had a thousand. He wasn't hurt, but he was dang sure in a bad way."

Another odd occurrence, as remembered by Harold Ray, was at the Herb Cahoon outside of Pittsburg. "The club officials were a little mixed up on their dinner and told us it was one day earlier than it actually was. I had my horses in a two-horse trailer on the grounds. We went to the dinner, which they didn't have that night, so we turned around and came back real early. I had a blanket on the horses, as it was pretty nasty weather. The next morning, I go out there and my horses were gone. I figured one of the trainers was playing a joke on me and had taken my horses out and hid them. When it came time to run my dogs, there were no horses around. That's when it got serious. I made one brace, came back in, and there was still no sign of the horses. I called the state police to keep a lookout, as the interstate was only five miles from the trial grounds. The state police said that if someone got them and they made it to the interstate, I was probably not going to see them again. Dr. Morgan had a friend in Pittsburg who had a helicopter. I got in the helicopter and started going around the country looking for them. The state had some acreage in the back of the trial grounds that was full of hedgerows. We went to this area, banked around, and I thought I could see a small bit of white in a thicket. I asked the pilot if he could land nearby. He did and sure enough there was a path cut into this thicket and there were my horses. That was the only time I had ever heard of horses being stolen at a field trial.

"Bruce Jacobs and I were pretty serious competitors against each other," Harold Ray said, telling this story as if it had happened yesterday. "He had a dog named Barnum who was the second dog to win the Norton Award. Sometimes Barnum would really hit his birds hard, and he would slide down. We were running at the North Carolina Championship. I was running a dog that looked just like ole Barnum. I'm riding up front just as happy as can be and see him jump down from his horse and style a dog up. He then gets back on his horse and calls point. We go riding up there, and Bruce is flushing. I said, 'Bruce, I believe that's my dog.' He hadn't gotten any birds up, so he didn't feel too bad. I got off my horse but didn't flush bird one."

This was an oddity for sure, as described by Shawn: "Awfully Amazing was running at the Quail Championship. During the brace, a hawk had dropped a bird on him. He started eating the bird during the competition. I knew not to stick my fingers in his mouth to retrieve the bird, so we just had to wait on him to finish eating."

"Training has been an evolution with me," Harold Ray shared after being asked about any special training tips. "Your training equipment and knowledge that has been passed down is not the answer to everything. For example, I don't use the hitch anymore. I don't even use the collar around the waist. My best advice is to work hard and try not to do it all in one session. One of the best friends I ever had was Stanley White. He was one of the best horse trainers in the world. At the end of his book, he wrote, 'Ask a lot and demand little.' When you think about it, that really says a lot. You can ask and ask and ask but the demand part is when you go beyond repetition and understanding and force it. When you start demanding, you are not training anymore."

Gordon Hazlewood would always relay this bit of wisdom to the trainers and helpers who went north with him: "You have to build a bond with a dog. If you have a dog that was a big running dog, which a lot of judges were looking for, you better be his best friend. You had to have him wanting to find you and not you go and find him. I told them that you can't go on the road and carry fifteen dogs and go to four or five field trials a month because sooner or later, you are going to go home with no money in your pocket. If you have got four or five really good dogs, that's where you ought to stay. Work those and go to field trials. If one of them is not quite good enough and you can find one that is better, then put the other one out and add the better one."

Along the same lines, Shawn Kinkelaar added, "Look for a dog that knows where you are at and one that will stay in front ten to two."

The final question asked of these highly successful trialers was what they cherished most in their field trial career. There were three outstanding replies.

"When I won all four placements in the New England Futurity with littermates was probably the height of my career," Harold Ray said proudly. "To win all four placements with littermates has not even come close to being done since. I also have to mention how fortunate I was to have the Smiths to work for. They were the greatest owners you could have. The Smiths would give you the opportunity to get rid of a dog if you felt like the dog was not going to make it. And if you were not winning with a dog and you thought you could, there was never any pressure to remove it from my string. They were the greatest."

Mr. Kinkelaar spoke quickly. "The eleven Dog of the Year awards. That was my goal when I set out, and to have that high a number is something I take pride in. I don't think anyone else has more than four or five."

"I won the National twice, won the Invitational one time, and won the Endurance three times as well as winning Dog of the Year twice. Winning these was very important to me. The thing I cherish most are the friendships I had, and still have, with so many people and owners. The friendships are more important to me than any of my accomplishments," said Gordon Hazlewood.

When contemplating the above comments, the lack of wild birds to trial on and the absence of youth in the pro ranks stand out. It is up to all of us to present our sport in a favorable way in order to attract new trialers and support research to preserve the bird that started it all. By doing so, we will leave the sport in good shape for the next generation. Many thanks to Gordon Hazelwood, Shawn Kinkelaar, and Harold Ray for their time and patience.

Gordon Hazelwood is congratulated after winning the 2002 Sunflower Open Shooting Dog Championship
Photo courtesy of Gordon Hazelwood

Harold Ray with Righteous Dan
Photo courtesy of Harold Ray

A Moment With One of the Best

Think of a circle. At the top is Elwin and Inez Smith. Moving clockwise, Harold Ray, the Smith Setters, Tomoka, and back to the top are the Smiths. There is no stopping point, just the endless circle: the Smiths, Mr. Ray, Smith Setters, and Tomoka. Around and around it goes; they cannot be separated. They are frozen in time in an endless circle, two Hall of Fame shooting dog and setter patrons, a Hall of Famer, master trainer and handler, a legendary line of setters, and one of the greatest setters the sport has ever known. This article is not just a casual conversation with Harold Ray, but rather his thoughts and insights about the Smiths, breeding, and a legendary dog that reminds us of the timeless spirit of field trials and our fascination with them.

Several years ago, Hoyle Eaton shared this with me: "If you keep breeding the best to the best of a certain line of dogs, sometime in the future the moon and stars will align, and you will get a throwback dog very close to its ancestors." I believe this happened with Shadow Oak Bo. If Shadow Oak Bo's pedigree is studied, the Smith setter line is woven tight into what this dog accomplished.

Mr. Ray began, "In the fall of 1958, I came down to Georgia and started working and training dogs with Fred Bevan. He gave me fifty dollars a month, but in the summer I had to chop cotton, as we didn't train dogs during that time of year. So you might say I started at the bottom. Mr. Smith had dogs with Fred. The Smiths' dogs, being shooting dogs and setters, opposed to all-age dogs, which he liked, were sort of like second-string dogs to him, so I got to work them. When Mr. Smith would come to look at the dogs, I would be the one showing them to him. At that time, I was considering quitting and mentioned that to Mr. Smith. He asked me to call him if I decided to quit, as he didn't want to leave his dogs there if I was not working with them. I quit not long afterward and did like he asked and gave him a call. There was a telephone booth in the Anthony Wayne hotel in Waynesboro that when you put a dollar of quarters in the slot, the money would go right through the phone and you could keep using the phone. So that's how I made my phone call without using my money. He asked me if I had a place to stay. I told Mr. Smith that we did not part on good terms, and I had not been paid and only had a total of three dollars to my name. When Mr. Smith asked me if I had a place to stay, the rates were three dollars a day, and I only had three dollars in my pocket, which I used for one night's lodging. From there he had someone pick me up, and that's how our relationship started.

"To tell you a story about Mr. Smith. We had some November pups, and I kept talking to Mr. Smith about making them January puppies. He went on for a while and never would answer me. Mr. Smith would not talk business in the field when we were working. If he had something to say about something that was going on, or something he didn't like or didn't understand, he wouldn't talk about it then. It would be two or three days later. I might say, 'How are things going?' and he would say, 'Stop by the house.' Then, when I would get there, he might say, 'You know the other day when you were working, I didn't quite understand why you did this or that.' He would always do this in a nice way. He was a great business man, and everybody loved him that worked for him. I was at his house one day and brought up the subject of the November puppies with him again. He looked at me and said that he knew that it would mean a lot to me, and he understood where I was coming from trial-wise if he would make these puppies January puppies. 'But I have never cheated in my business and damn sure not going to cheat in my hobby.' And that was never mentioned again.

"Mr. Smith did not give judges favors nor did he believe in giving free hunts, doing any entertaining, or giving a pup away to gain favoritism. He didn't play the game from that perspective.

"The Smiths would keep a list of names they liked and then compile it. Before we would register puppies, we wanted to make sure they had a good chance to make it. When we registered them, we would go over the list of names and find a name that suited that particular dog. In the case of Tomoka, they were in Arizona on a trip and saw this name they really liked, which was Tomoka. In Arizona, which has a large Native American population, the name Tomoka means Little Chief. So when John, Tomoka's call name, was a standout dog as a puppy, he was given the name Tomoka.

"Mr. Smith picked the dogs to work as puppies and told me, 'You be careful with this one; he's a good one.' Even with a bad back, he would get on a tractor and run the puppies. He was a good amateur handler, knew dogs, was a hunter, and liked to run his own dogs. Mr. Smith leased Di-Lane Plantation just to hunt on. The place I am on now was bought at a tax sale by Mr. Smith, who paid cighteen dollars an acre for it. The dog business was a family thing; both of the Smiths did it together.

"I was blessed to have people like the Smiths to work for. A dog and trainer are no better than the owners. They made me a better trainer. Mr. and Mrs. Smith would not buy dogs. They raised and trialed their own puppies. If I messed one up, then I would have to wait two years for another. There were no deadlines I had to meet. If I didn't want to keep a dog, they would get rid of it. Even if a dog wasn't winning and I said this dog is going to win, they would stick with me and the dog. I have always said give me a good owner and

I'll get him a good dog. They were the reason the Smith Setters were so successful. Because of their attitude and their staying power. Without the Smiths and their contributions to the setter world, there would not be a Shadow Oak Bo. That pretty much sums up their legacy.

"A trait of the Smith dogs is that they are not hyper dogs in the kennel and very calm and quiet. Another trait is that they are clean in the kennel. The Smith Setters were not like a lot of setters that you would see in the early days—and even today—that are really hyper and busy. You take Susan's Lady Bird, Tomoka's dam, you would never know she was in the kennel. No jumping and barking. She wasn't even one to play with a feathered wing. She was just business. There was no butterfly stuff. She was just like an old dog as a puppy.

"When I started working for Mr. Smith, I was getting 150 dollars a month. I wasn't getting rich, but I was happy. His dogs were running in grouse trials, so therefore I had to go to those trials. Carl Barkley, who broke Grouse Ridge John and Grouse Ridge Will, worked for Tom Flanagan. We would move from Georgia to Pennsylvania and from there back to Georgia and in the mid-summer to Canada. Mr. Smith had a cottage in Pennsylvania where Sherry and I and Carl and his wife lived. There were times that we would put all our money together just to buy a bucket of fried chicken. We actually hunted grouse for food. Carl hunted Grouse Ridge John, who sired two Hall of Fame dogs, Grouse Ridge Will and Tomoka, and I hunted Highlander's Duffy. Carl had a slight speech impediment and he would call them 'groose birds.'

"Both dogs were extremely stylish and didn't have faults. They pointed birds, backed, and were very intense on their game. When you put the two together, you were not breeding faults. The first litter of pups we had from Highlander Duffy and Skylight's Susan produced Susan's Lady Bird, So High, Tomoka, and Duffy's Moon Maid, which is the dam of Cash Master. I really wanted to breed Susan's Ladybird to Grouse Ridge John. Ladybird and John were very much alike. Our dogs always crossed real good with Dr.

Flanagan's dogs. They were great bird dogs, had great natural abilities, and naturally ran to the front like all good grouse dogs. These dogs we are talking about all figure prominently in Shadow Oak Bo's pedigree. These traits breed true. I've seen and judged Bo several times, and he only had two things on his mind: running to the front and finding birds. That's what wins field trials. I never believed in breeding faults. I bred the best to the best. If a dog didn't win, Mr. Smith wouldn't breed it. His reasoning for that was each dog had to prove that they could take training. There are a lot of pretty pups out there who just can't take training. Mr. Smith only bred his very best females. When Susan's Lady Bird was young, I was winning derby and puppy stakes with her. She was my first champion. Grouse Ridge John had no natural faults. There was no squatting or flagging. He could find birds; it was just unreal. These dogs go back to CH Sam LS Sky High and then back to Sky High. One thing about Sky High was he was an extremely powerful and classy dog. Back then, the grouse trials were two-hour trials, which meant you needed a rather tough dog.

If a dog comes from behind twice in a grouse trial, you might as well pick him up. To win in a grouse trial, you have to have three things: First, the dog had to stay in front of you. Second, the dog had to be very classy, and third, the dog had to point grouse. It was almost in that order, as the birds were very scarce. The judges would see the dogs running a lot more than pointing. Therefore, these dogs were good front running dogs.

"Four of the pups in Tomoka's litter were field trial winners. In that litter was So High. Mr. Smith won a lot of amateur trials with him. Another was Amber. I won the 1976 Prairie Chicken Championship with her and the South Carolina Shooting Dog Classic in 1974. When we crossed I'm Oscar and the Smith dogs, such as the breeding of I'm Oscar to Amber, that just kept us in dogs forever. That was the main line that we had. Breeding these two produced Pinnacle . . . Look on the top side of Shadow Oak Bo x Shak Ti x Cooters Carolina Casey x Carolina Cooter Man, who is out of Pinnacle. Duffy's Moon Maid, another pup in the litter, produced Cash Master.

"Tomoka was a July puppy. All the dogs that are going to be derbies that coming year I gang ran together. I had some full all-age coming derbies plus these July pups, Tomoka, Amber, So High, and Duffy's Moon Maid. I was gang running them one day and, of course, the older puppies were running bigger. Coming from an all-age background and being mentally all age–oriented, I loved a big running dog. I probably had twelve to fifteen pups on the ground and noticed Tomoka standing at a bush looking up and pointing. All the other dogs were running around and past him. I thought, 'look at that crazy dog.' Then I saw a small bird nest in the top of the bush. The bush was about five foot high and most of the leaves had fallen off. I just left him standing there and kept looking back as I moved forward. All of a sudden he jumped into the bush, and at the base of the bush was an old hen with a bunch of little ones. He was the only dog out of the bunch that could smell the birds. That gets your attention. The pups in the litter all had good noses, but his was exceptional. At that time, I wasn't even considering breaking him, as he was such an off-age puppy. That summer I had some Japanese visitors staying with me that wanted to work dogs. I thought it would be best if they worked John and Amber. One of the Japanese fellows was running John when he pointed. The birds were flushed and flew right into John's face, and he chased them. When this happened, I turned my horse, and by accident the horse stepped on the rope and flipped him and that dog was broke from then on. I won the pheasant Futurity with him when he was fourteen months old. I had two finds with him with Gene Galloway and Rich Tuttle judging. They said on one of his finds he had the greatest relocation they had ever seen a dog do. He just had that ability. He would never lose contact with the bird, and he always knew where they were. He never put his head down and just didn't make mistakes. Everything was just so easy for him.

"Tomoka was a very quiet dog. There was no running around or barking in the kennel. He may have been calm in the kennel, but when you turned him loose, he was all business in the field. Even when he had a dog running all around him, he would never lose concentration on the bird scent. He had the whole package of intensity. It wasn't just his head not moving, his whole body was that way.

"It's what's in a dog's breeding. That sums up Tomoka. All a trainer can do is bring out the capabilities of that animal. Back then, I only had about twelve dogs, and they were worked, they were worked, and they were worked. At a young age, they had probably seen more birds than most derby dogs. We just about had an unlimited amount of birds in Canada, and the amount of birds they saw brought out what they were capable of doing. On wild birds, a dog learns to go to the body scent of those birds and figure it out. When I am looking at young dogs and running them all together, I can sort out time after time the dogs you are going to win with. I kept a record of every workout, the length of the workout, and what the dog did during the workout. I wrote down every unproductive, every stop to flush, whether they flagged or laid down, no matter what it was, I kept a complete record. At the end of the summer, I went over the record of all of the dogs, and if they didn't have a performance that would win a field trial, I would quit them. It's hard to be honest. I cull hard; I just don't sugarcoat it. You have to cull hard to win big.

"When Tomoka won the Georgia Shooting Dog Championship, it was hot, and we had the first brace after dinner. In Georgia, trying to find wild birds in the middle of the day is not the time to win field trials. At Di-Lane Plantation, you have a bunch of wet-weather ponds and swamp creeks. The birds have to come out of these places for you to have any luck at all. I told Sherry to stay in camp, and I'd get Jim Sorrels to scout for me; we are not going to win anyway as hot as it is. I turned John loose, and he was just having find after find. That night we got sixteen inches of snow, and the trial didn't resume for another week.

"The last trial he ran in was at Rend Lake. After this trial, I was going to retire him. I think after his third find he was pointed, and just before I got there, he jumped in and knocked the bird and chased it off. I gathered him up, petted him, and put him in a harness. It was kinda like him saying, 'This one is for me.' "

I would like to thank Mr. Harold Ray for taking the time to visit with me. His memories intrigue us while his knowledge helps us make our dogs better.

Harold Ray with his first Champion Susan's Lady Bird
Photo courtesy of Harold Ray

Elwin Smith, Harold Ray, Inez Smith and Champion Touch of Class

Photo courtesy of Harold Ray

Tommy Olive Remembers

Tommy Olive was destined to play an integral part in the golden age of field trials. He was placed by providence in just the right spot at the right time, with the right people, to have hands-on experience with arguably the greatest pointer of all time. The greats of the sport he idolized as a boy and then trialed with as an adult are growing fewer by the year and beg not to be forgotten. Mr. Olive's time with the sport did not encompass a lifetime but did leave an impact that will live on for years to come. Today, Mr. Olive helps blow the dust off the field trial bible of years gone by to recount precious memories as if they happened yesterday.

"I grew up hunting with my uncle and another guy who was kind of like my daddy. He had beagle dogs, and my uncle had bird dogs. I was following them around when I was six years old and remember my uncle's dogs pointing, him handing me his twelve-gauge and then telling me to kill a bird. I walked up and shot, hit the ground, and the birds kept going. After that trip, I got a bird dog on my own and trained him all by myself.

"My family had a small dairy farm and sold milk to the locals. Mr. Dick Brown, a Booneville businessman, was a regular customer. Mr. Brown started noticing my dog and wanted to know who trained him. I said, 'Well, nobody did. I just got him to doing some stuff.' The little dog was almost all white, just like White Knight. He wanted to see him point some birds, so I took him out, and he couldn't believe it. He said, 'You need to be in the bird dog business!' I was still pretty young at the time and thought he was just paying me a compliment. When I got a little bit older, he came out and again told me I needed to get into the bird dog business. During that time frame, he brought a dog to me, and I trained it for him. That's basically the way I started, as Dick Brown, Hoyle Eaton, and Billy Morton were all good friends and friends of mine."

Mr. Olive rubbed shoulders with some of the best handlers and dogs to ever run in field trials. Mr. Jimmy Potter of Selma, Arkansas, recounted a conversation he had with Mr. Olive many years ago concerning the training of Red Water Rex and Riggins White Knight, which led to the following: when asked about wild bird hunting these two National champions while working for Hoyle Eaton, Mr. Olive laughed and replied, "It's something I did with all dogs. If you were down on the ground with them pointing birds, killing birds, and making them retrieve, it just seemed like it did something for those dogs. That's the way I always trained mine before I even thought about a field trial. I continued it right into a dog's field trial career. Sometimes Hoyle didn't like what I did, but when he found out it was working, he changed his mind completely. When Red Water Rex pointed, he got everyone's attention; he was such a great dog to look at. I think a lot of that came from me bird hunting him on foot. After I started bird hunting him, I hardly ever had to get on to that dog at all. He was very laid back, but in a trial, Rex was bound and determined to find more birds than the dog he was braced with. You could tell it by looking at him.

"Of the dogs I campaigned, the one that stands out was a young dog owned by Mr. Henry Berol called Berol's Paul Gundy. Mr. Berol owned Di-Lane Plantation in Georgia when I went to work for him. He had wanted me to come over there for years. I really believe that

I could have won the National with that dog. There is no doubt in my mind. He was the top qualifying dog the first time I ran him at the Continental. Those birds down there in the finals get mean late in the day, and I think I was the last dog to draw. The birds were flying on him, and he jumped and cost me going to the National with him the very first year. He was a super-great dog. When Mr. Berol passed away, they told me I would be able to keep the kennel open. Very shortly after his passing, I had the flu for about two weeks, and when I was better, his wife closed the kennel and sold the dog. One of the judges bought him, and the dog was run over and killed at one of the eastern trials. He looked a lot like Red Water Rex and had his characteristics. He was as good a bird dog as I ever rode a horse behind."

As with interviews with Hoyle Eaton and Billy Morton, Mr. Olive's voice sharpened when asked about Riggins White Knight. "Riggins White Knight was by far the smartest dog I have ever seen or heard of. Before he ever ran in a field trial, we had taken him to a veterinarian in Baldwin, Mississippi, where he was going to spend the night in his office. He was by himself in the office when came a severe lightning storm. He got out of his cage, busted out a plate-glass window, chewed through a cyclone fence, went across Highway 45, was cut all to pieces, and managed to find somebody to help him. Soon as they saw the dog, they called the vet, and he got him back to the clinic and sewed him up. From that day on, because he was by himself when the storm came, he had to ride with us in the cab of the pickup and sleep with either me or Hoyle in the bed.

"He was just like a kid to me and Hoyle. You could take him to a field trial and stay in a motel room, go back the next year to the same motel, and he would remember the room we stayed in the previous year. An instance that sticks in my mind was Carbondale, Illinois. They would make the field trialers park in the back because of the trucks. When we got there, I just let ole Bud out because he would walk beside you wherever you went. When we went in a glass door to get into the motel, Bud went all the way down the hall and was waiting on us by the room we had stayed the year before. To top it off, Joe Hurdle had watched him run many a time, and he accused me of riding him on my saddle after he was getting older. It actually cost him winning a field trial. I told him, 'Mr. Hurdle, I promise you I did not ever have Bud on my saddle.' He said, 'Why was he gone so long, and when you came back he was right behind you?' I tried to explain to him how I had caught that dog hiding behind a tree resting when he got so old that he couldn't stay in front of the gallery like he wanted to. He would rest a minute or two and then come out wide open. This happened several times. One time was west of Saint Louis, Missouri, where they had the old bunkers for the army. The last year Bud ran, he would go around behind those bunkers and take a rest. When I would ride past him, he would take off for the front again. Riggins White Knight was amazing. It didn't make any difference if it was blizzard conditions or so hot you could hardly breathe, he was one of the only dogs I ever saw that would not even hesitate or slow up. When other dogs would slow up, he just wouldn't. He was that determined to please people. He was just a one hundred-percent people dog.

"Red Water Rex was not a totally different dog, but he didn't go burning the field up like Riggins White Knight did. White Knight had one speed, and that was wide open. Rex would pace himself, and he was a smart enough dog that he could tell when he was getting too hot or he was having trouble. And you could notice him slow down just a little bit, but it would never keep him from finding birds. He would still go out there and point as many or more birds than any dog in existence. He just had a different demeanor to him, and I guess it was like having one kid that liked to be wide open and run a hundred miles an hour all the time and having another kid that would like to stop and think about what he was doing. That's one way I always thought about them. They were very temperamental dogs, but above all, both of them wanted to please. That was very unusual to have two dogs like that in one kennel.

"There was a puppy out of Bud that I think would have been better than him; his name was White Knight's Bullet. He came down with something in his blood that the veterinarians at Auburn University could not identify, and he died real young."

White Knight's Bullet's dam was Bar Lane Dot. In his short career, he placed eleven times, with notable wins in the 1965 Border International Derby, 1967 Missouri Open, 1967 Southwestern, and the 1968 Quail Championship. It is not known how many litters he sired, but at least two of his get were registered: Haberdasher's Mary and Wild Becky.

As far as a performance to remember, Mr. Olive put Red Water Rex and Riggins White Knight up there with the best when they won the National Championship. "When Riggins White Knight won the National, it was bitter, bitter cold. During that cold snap, for some reason, the dogs absolutely could not smell birds. I found ole Bud twice pointing in gullies that were fifteen or twenty-foot deep. How in the world that dog could get down in those gullies, find birds, point, then me be lucky enough to find him, I'll never know. The finds in the gullies were when you could really see the gallery and the judges perk up. That's when I knew we had it won. Rex did not have the stamina of White Knight, but he had a way of coming alive toward the end of a brace and streak in front of the gallery. I think it comes from a determination that not all dogs possess. It was instilled in both Rex and White Knight, where they just would not quit. Sometimes in Canada, I'd have to run a horse half to death to pick them up and stop them from running."

When asked about interesting stories, these two stood out. "In the late summer after breaking camp in Canada, we would stop in Silver Springs, Wisconsin, and run a trial. It was on the way back home and gave us a break from the long drive back. We had a dog running in a brace, and the cover was thick. I had my horse going, and when I say going, I mean going. All of a sudden, a black bear ran out of the bushes straight in front of me, the horse went airborne, and how I stayed on him, I'll never know. Another story was at a trial in Carbondale, Illinois. I was running a dog, and the course was very muddy. The dog had been lost, and I was trying to get back in front of the gallery, which had made its way about a half mile in front of me. The horse and dog were running wide open when the horse stepped in a gopher hole and started down. For some reason, when I started down on the right side, the saddle caught my leg. The horse did a flip and landed right on top of me. The only reason it didn't kill me was because the ground was muddy. The calf of my leg was tore in two, and I had a couple of broken ribs. When it happened, the dog stopped and came back and then both of them took off and left me out there.

"I was so lucky during my field trial days as all of us worked together as a team. We got along with each other, and I think pretty much everybody. Mr. Dick Brown had a big part in the success of the three of us. We all knew each other's families and went to each other's houses and ate together all the time. In one sense, it was just a big family."

Many thanks to Mr. Tommy Olive for taking the time to share his stories and knowledge of a time of legendary dogs and their handlers.

Tommy Olive and Hoyle Eaton with White Knight
Photo courtesy of Tommy Olive

Tommy Olive, Hoyle Eaton and judge Joe Hurdle inspect Riggins White Knight after his brace in frigid conditions at the National. "Bud" had run his pads off.
Photo courtesy of Tommy Olive

One In Ten Thousand

The hope—the anticipation—of the next great dog burns within the soul of all good bird dog men and women. Finding that 1 in 10,000 prospect that pulls us out of a warm bed in the morning and tucks us in at night with dreams of what can be. We seek that dog, the one whose style and grace paints upon a lifetime canvas the memories of the young and makes the old again feel the exuberance of their youth. This happened to Hoyle Eaton at a truly unexpected time in his life—a time not to mount up against younger handlers for one last shot at glory but a time to retire. Lightning had struck out of a blue sky, and a pup to be named Sir Lancelot was staring out of the kennel into Mr. Eaton's eyes causing him to think, "What if?"

Sir Lancelot was sired by Miraculous ex Townson's Little Jody.

"I don't breed to dogs just on their name. I breed to dogs on their qualities," Mr. Eaton stated. "If I liked a dog, then I would go see what his breeding was. The pedigree does not determine how I breed dogs."

Eaton had seen some impressive pups by Miraculous, had also trialed him for a short time, and thought another shot at this breeding was in order. He leased the pup's dam with the litter producing not only Sir Lancelot but Lester's Leeza, the dam of National Champion Lester's Snowatch.

Lancelot was whelped on June 2, 2001 at Hoyle Eaton's kennel. When asked why he selected this pup out of the litter, Eaton replied, "He was a pretty white pup, but as he grew, he had that championship look, a unique, beautiful dog. His demeanor was that of a winner. When he got to be about four months old, I would take him out. He began to get in shape and looked good running. I would see him stack up behind snipe and point them twelve o'clock. He just had the overall look of a champion."

Lancelot spent a portion of the summer of his Derby season in upper Michigan working on chicken. Much of his training from six months to a year was spent at Hell Creek. "Sometimes I would leave him down four hours or maybe a little more," said Mr. Eaton. "He would never quit and was always bird hunting. It was a pleasure to be in the field with him."

Hoyle Eaton thought that Sir Lancelot was a "throwback." He had shared his thoughts on genetics with the author several years ago. It was Mr. Eaton's belief that over a period of years and many breedings, the DNA would again align just right, cause a throwback to come forward and produce a dog very close to an ancestor.

"Sir Lancelot was about a clone of Riggins White Knight," Mr. Eaton stated. "He was a bit bigger, but everything else was a clone. The way they ran the country and the way they went bird hunting, intelligence, and the way they handled was truly amazing to me."

Many feel that Lancelot was possibly the greatest Derby of our generation. Bill Stubblefield judged him in one of his first Derby wins. "He was a beautiful dog, and even back when he was real young he was just a remarkable dog. He was so light of foot that he would stride like he was hardly hitting the ground. I will never forget that trial and the caliber of dog he was."

Bobby McAlexander, who has judged the last eight renewals of the National Championship at Grand Junction, said, "Sir Lancelot knew what he was out there for and ran with a purpose: to find birds. He had a really smooth fluid gait, could go for one or three hours, and wanted to please his handler. He looked excellent on his game and was one of the most beautiful dogs on point that I had ever seen. And that was most every time he pointed! He ran strong, to the front, and was smart and birdy. He was more mature than most Derby dogs and wasn't just 'puppying' around. Sir Lancelot was special, and the best young dog that I had ever seen."

Mr. Eaton believes one of the greatest hour performances by a Derby he had ever been a part of was when Lancelot pointed seven coveys in the Hobart Ames Open All-Age at Grand Junction in 2002.

Tom Word reported the 2003 National Derby Championship at Sedgefields Plantation for The American Field, which Sir Lancelot won.

"White Knight, bred by the young man from Mississippi, launched the distinguished handling career of D. Hoyle Eaton. This year, at 73 years of age, he returned to compete in the National Derby Championship with a homebred white Derby that traces many times to White Knight and to Eaton's other landmark dogs, Red Water Rex and Ormond Smart Alec. Again, he and the pointer won it convincingly with an ambitious three-find performance where he showed great intelligence and understanding of game and the use of the breeze to locate. His finds came at 17, 40, and 50. Intelligence was the word used by both Eaton and Judge Wayne Mauldin in describing Sir Lancelot."

Another major championship for Lancelot was the United States Open in 2004. Lancelot ran the sixth brace; the weather was overcast and warm with a breeze. He was braced with Peacemaker in the sixth brace. Heather Klinck reported for The American Field that "The dogs were loosed near the crossroads. At 4, Lancelot pointed on our right. His tall stature was complemented by a high head and tail as the birds were flushed in front of him. Just two minutes later, scout David Shoemaker called point, and a large covey was flushed for him. He added to the first two finds by others at 16, 24, and at 26, which required Mr. Eaton to relocate him. His last find was far to the front, totaling six finds."

Lancelot's record shows eight first place wins: Hell Creek Open Derby, 2002; Tootsie Hurdle Open Derby, 2002; National Derby Championship, 2003; Dixie Field Trial Open Derby, 2003; United States Open, 2004; Blackbelt Open All-Age, 2004; Tootsie Hurdle Open All-Age, 2004; Tootsie Hurdle Open All- Age, 2006.

Other placements included the Tootsie Hurdle Open All-Age, 2nd, 2003; Hobart Ames Open All-Age, 2nd, 2004; Dixie Field Trial Club Open All-Age, 2nd, 2004; Hobart Ames Memorial Open All-Age, 2nd, 2005 and the Hell Creek Open All-Age, 3rd, 2008.

Without question the heartbreak of Sir Lancelot's career came at the 2005 National Championship at Grand Junction. He had amassed ten finds during the first two hours and 45 minutes and had just pointed No. 11.

Dale Bush, judging that day, said: "His performance in the 2005 National Championship was one of the greatest dog showings I have ever seen. Every time Hoyle turned him loose after a find, he would go straight to the front, out of sight, and the next time we would see him, he would be on point. He did all this while hardly getting any mud on him. As history now knows, as we were riding to him on his last find, we started riding single birds up, and they started flying over him one at a time and finally he broke and chased.

"For two hours and forty-five minutes, it was something to see. Had he not broke, they could have run for months and not have a performance like that."

Bobby McAlexander, who was riding in the gallery, recalled, "The dog was really getting the job done. The excitement was there with the gallery. The dog was just out of pocket, and Mr. Eaton had gone back to look for him as he popped out to the front and soon pointed. When David Shoemaker started off his horse to flush the birds, Lancelot took them out. It was a heartbreaker for everyone . . . The gallery was in awe of what happened."

Mr. Eaton had wanted to end his career with a win at the National, and he very nearly did.

"It would have been interesting to know what his career and winning record would have been had I been twenty years younger, and had my longtime scout Robert Burris," Mr. Eaton offered. "If this were the case, the bird dog world might very well recognize Sir Lancelot as a National Champion and the winner of several other major championships."

A true mark of a great dog is name recognition. Few in the field trial world would fail to recognize the name Sir Lancelot. That name is forever associated with Hoyle Eaton, just as are Riggins White Knight and Red Water Rex. When style and grace are discussed among trialers, it is a safe bet that Sir Lancelot will be mentioned with the great dogs of today and the past. His intelligence and bird-finding ability were second to none during the years of 2002 through 2005, which was the heart of his trialing. The field trial community should be grateful to Mr. Eaton for recognizing the potential of this fine dog and accomplishing what few have done at his age. Sir Lancelot's legacy lives on through his progeny—currently 100 winners with 383 wins—a tribute to a truly remarkable dog.

D. Hoyle Eaton with Sir Lancelot
Photo courtesy of the author

✣ STORIES ✣

A Symphony of Tears
Puddin
Three Cups of Coffee
The Bond
The Wolves of Crow Mountain
Heaven
The Christmas Present

A Symphony of Tears

John Robinson's proudest day was the birth of his son, Dan. The doctor's news that the child had Down's syndrome did not seem to faze him in the least. John and his wife Linda had tried for many years to have a child, and now they were blessed with Dan. When John held little Dan for the first time, the bond was cemented between father and son. So a life begins and also our story.

For fourteen years, John had been training and trialing dogs for just three families. He knew without a shadow of a doubt he had the best owners in the business. John was especially fond of an old gentleman from Arkansas named Jimmy Gennings. Jimmy was a retired army one-star general whose opinions were some of the most respected in the field trial world. He and his wife had never had children. His eyes sparkled when telling others he had known John from a pup, as John's father had also trained dogs for him. Mr. Gennings never looked at Dan as if he had a disability, but rather with an eye for the opportunity to share life with another member of the Robinson family.

As little Dan grew, he and his dad were inseparable. If John was in the saddle, so was Dan, riding in his dad's arms. If the dogs required yard work, then both the Robinsons, father and son, were at the task. They sat beside each other at the dinner table and there were few times the truck left without Dan in it.

Dan went to Canada each year with his parents and a string of dogs. His mother, Linda, kept a close eye on him. The drive to Canada each year was always punctuated by an afternoon service station stop and a pop and candy bar. John noticed some of the stares at Dan but he never let on to Linda and especially not to Dan. He would say, "Dan, you are my best friend, you and your mom are the loves of my life." Dan would always hug John and say, "I love you too, Pop."

At the age of nine and beyond, Dan's main job was official puppy trainer. Dan loved socializing the puppies and would spend hours with them in the fenced in area behind their Canadian cabin. He was very comfortable with the puppies and importantly, they were comfortable with him.

Dan's tenth summer on the prairies was special. He was allowed to ride in the saddle with his dad over the endless sea of grass. This was in addition to his job with the puppies and with visiting with the friends and clients of his dad who dropped by to visit. It was a special event for all when Mr. Jimmy Gennings would arrive in camp. Jolly, smiling, a bit overweight, Gennings was warm with Southern charm and had an unmistakable laugh that told Dan his good buddy had arrived.

One day after a late afternoon gully washer, Dan could not to be found. It was all hands on deck to search, with Mr. Gennings finally finding him. Dan had made his way into a big dog house in the puppy pen when the rain started. He was doing his job as puppy trainer. He then fell asleep with all the puppies either in his lap or laying close to him. Mr. Gennings quietly brought John and Linda to a good angle to see inside the puppy house. There was Dan, still asleep with his little charges. John smiled as Linda gripped John's arm and held close while shedding a few tears of relief, love, and happiness. Mr. Gennings looked at the husband

and wife, then at Dan, and felt a warm contentment come over him, knowing he was with people he loved.

On Dan's sixteenth birthday, John gave him the tamest, most easy-going, gentlest horse he could find. Dan took to riding like a duck to water and was now able to attend field trials with his dad. John was always careful to make sure he had a supervisor riding next to him. There was never a question of his safety. Around this time, Dan was given more responsibility around the dogs. During training sessions, Dan would dismount with his dad, style the dogs up, help flush birds, and shoot the training pistol upon the flush. He was taught how to leash and unleash the dogs and how to send them to the front. The things he did had been learned from keeping a watchful eye on John and his training methods.

Often Mr. Gennings would accompany the two Robinsons on the prairie. He would ride next to Dan and enjoy his youthful exuberance. In watching Dan mature, Mr. Gennings gained even more respect for John as a father and man. One day while sitting on the porch with John, Mr. Gennings looked John straight in the eye and said, "I can't imagine how Dan could have a better father than you. You are truly the son I never had."

It took John a long minute to reply, "Dan is all I ever dreamed of as a son and you have been, and always will be, a member of our family."

Enough was said. The two men went back to discussing derbies, training methods and how good Linda's fried chicken supper smelled, the scent of which slowly drifted from the kitchen to the porch.

That night in bed at camp on the prairie, John looked at Dan, who was sleeping, and gave thanks to the Lord for his son.

For nigh-on thirty years, Mr. Gennings had been looking, hoping, and praying for a dog that would rise with the cream to the top of the field trial world. A Hall of Fame, National Championship caliber dog. He hoped he had finally found such a dog in Thunder. An imposing liver and white pointer male who could cover ground and leave a fire behind. Thunder had belonged to Mr. Gennings since a pup. He could wind a bird in the next county and would handle after the initial cast after breakaway. Thunder was a pup whom Dan had socialized, loved, and picked out for Mr. Gennings.

Thunder qualified for the National, winning a trial on the prairies. Mr. Gennings was beside himself enjoying the people and festivities that went along with attending the National Championship as an owner. John was quietly optimistic. He and Dan, now eighteen, rode every brace before Thunder was drawn to run, the last brace of the final day. Birds at Ames were neither plentiful nor scarce that year. Three dogs had tallied six finds and much discussion centered around which one of these three would be crowned champion barring a spectacular performance in the last brace.

Dan was a favorite at field trials. He knew everyone and everybody knew him. Personable, outgoing, and well-mannered, he was always met with waves and greetings where ever he traveled in the field trial world. This year's National was no exception. Finally, the morning of the last brace came. John and Dan made ready. It was important to Dan to be dressed just like his dad—same clothes, check; whistle, check; trial pistol, check. Both Robinsons were ready to go. Dan was given the honor of releasing Thunder at the break-away and the brace was on. John rode up front as was customary with Dan riding at the front of the gallery with a nervous Mr. Gennings. Dan comforted Mr. Gennings by saying, "Don't worry, Mr. Gennings, Thunder and Dad know what to do."

Mr. Gennings replied, "I know, son, but it doesn't keep me from worrying."

One find for Thunder, then two and three, the first hour came to a close with Thunder running the brace of his life. John's heart pounded with each find, knowing that, barring a mistake or breach of manners, the National might be in his grasp.

At 1:25, Thunder's bracemate was picked up and the gallery began to sense that the National might be Thunder's to win or lose. Three more perfect finds with Thunder appearing to the front at just the right time for the judges, and the fact that he was on fire running and penning birds, added to the drama and excitement for all involved. Another find at 2:30, and Mr. Gennings was beside himself, checking his pocket watch with almost each passing minute. Hoping that the judges would call time before a mistake was made. Suddenly, at 2:45, a heavy, drenching, cold rainstorm hit. It rained so hard that it impaired visibility.

At 2:50, Thunder did not show to the front. The gallery suddenly became quiet. Was Thunder on point? Had the driving rain so impaired visibility that the dog might not be found? Could he be located in time for history to be made? All these thoughts and more buzzed around Dan and Mr. Gennings. A lifetime of work depended on these few precious minutes that were left. John had a feeling that Thunder had not made the last turn and proceeded with his scout, with the permission of the judges, to search to the left.

John said a short prayer as he used every instinct and bit of knowledge he possessed to find Thunder and either call point or bring him to the front and the possible championship. As he disappeared into the pelting rain, the judges came to an abrupt halt. There, not twenty yards to the front, standing like a proud statue, was Thunder, barely visible through the brush and rain. John was not within hearing distance as the rain and accompanying wind were as loud as an eighteen wheeler. Would the birds hold or run? What would Thunder do after such a perfect brace? There was nothing to do but wait, wish, and worry as Mr. Gennings could feel the lifelong dream of winning a National slipping away with each drop of cold rain. If only John would reappear through the storm. If only.

To Mr. Gennings's dismay, when glancing to his right to check on Dan, he saw he was no longer in the saddle but moving toward Thunder with pistol in hand. Just seconds before one of the judges was going to stop Dan, Mr. Gennings caught the senior judge's eye and motioned to leave the boy alone. Since Mr. Gennings was the owner and so well respected, the judge honored his request. Dan struggled slowly through the brush and sharp thorns just like he had done hundreds of times with his father. Closer and closer toward Thunder he moved until he passed his canine friend, seven feet in front and the birds lifted.

Right at that moment, John rode to the front of the gallery in time to see Dan fire his pistol. Thunder never moved a muscle and the judges called time. As Dan made his way toward John, one of the judges started to applaud, then the gallery, one by one, began clapping until the sound formed a perfect symphony with the rhythm of the rain drops in tribute to Thunder and Dan. John's face was wet not with rain but with tears, tears for a son he loved and tears for the hopes and dreams of a little baby he lovingly held in his arms not so many years ago. Linda, who had been riding in the gallery, joined the pair. The three hugged and rejoiced in a true miracle of the joy of life. Mr. Gennings sat in silence, cherishing the moment, knowing he had witnessed history which would be remembered forever in National Championship lore.

Not far from a dry trailer, Dan turned and addressed John, "Thunder must have done a great job; everyone clapped at the end of his brace."

John spent a moment in deep thought and then replied, "They were clapping for both you and Thunder."

Dan looked puzzled and said, "Why me?"

John turned toward Dan, patted him on the back, and replied, "Because you are my son and I love you."

Dan shook his head, took a deep breath, and said, "This has been the best day of my life. I will always love you, Pop."

Thunder was indeed crowned National Champion. The caption under the image in the American Field read: "Dan Robinson, handler with National Champion, Gennings Rolling Thunder. Back row: owner Jimmy Gennings and proud parents John and Linda Robinson."

Dedicated to my good friend, James Bronson. A lover of people, apple pie, bird dog puppies, and field trials.

Puddin

All his life, John "Puddin" Lacy had watched Mr. Ike Moore drive by in a truck loaded to the gills with enough dogs to fill a kennel. His parents' shotgun house faced the dusty gravel road that carried the plantation traffic. Mr. Ike was employed by the Yancopin Plantation of French Camp, Mississippi, as assistant manager but, more importantly, as chief dog trainer. He was the only man the plantation's owner, Mr. Charles King, trusted to handle his dogs in the major circuit field trials.

Puddin was five-foot-one, skinny, with a smile that could light up the darkest night. His nickname came from his love of banana pudding. His after-school job on the plantation entailed washing Mr. King's Cadillac, mowing and raking the plantation house's yard, and greeting guests when they arrived. Never to meet a stranger, Puddin, with his big smile, was without a doubt one of Mr. King's favorite employees.

Mr. Ike was known by all in the field trial circuit. Likable, hardworking, weathered, and Sunday-honest. He had trained and handled two National Champions and too many winners of other trials to count. He was fifty-three and looked every bit of it. It was nearing July 1, 1951, and Mr. Ike was making final preparations for the long trip to the Canadian prairies. Puddin had assisted Mr. Ike with loading for previous journeys north and secretly wanted to go, as he had never ventured more than twenty miles away from the shotgun house, cotton fields, and pine hills he knew as home.

Finally working up the nerve, he blurted out the question, "Mr. King, sir, if I can be spared from my plantation duties," he paused and took a deep breath, "could I go north to the prairies with Mr. Ike?" He also hoped Mr. King would ask Mr. Ike for him. Mr. King chewed on the question for what seemed to Puddin an eternity, turned, and said, "I think it's a dandy idea." Later that day Mr. King did indeed discuss the idea with Ike. Ike said he had all the help he needed, but at Mr. King's insistence he grudgingly relented and agreed to take Puddin along. Mr. King said, "Ike, there is something special about Puddin. I think you will agree after spending some time with him."

A week later, just before daybreak, with only a faint orange reminder of the sunrise to come, off went the Moore training crew in a new 1951 green Chevrolet truck followed by a red 1948 Ford. Ike, the camp cook, and dogs were in one truck; Puddin, two helpers, a few dogs, and lots of supplies were in another. His mother had carefully packed his belongings: four shirts, three pairs of pants, and a few toilet items in a large paper bag. They headed northwest through Mississippi cotton country, Memphis, and the Missouri bootheel. Puddin was wide-eyed, as he had never ventured out of Choctaw county, much less the state of Mississippi. There were hills, trees, fields, and mobs of people all in a rush to get from here to there. The world was certainly bigger and much different than what he had envisioned while sitting and dreaming on the small front porch attached to his family's house.

The first night was spent just off the highway on a friendly farmer's property. Hungry dogs were staked out and fed first. Then, supper for the crew. The cook was an older man in his middle sixties nicknamed "Spoon." Spoon had made fifteen trips to the prairie with Mr. Ike and was reputed to be the best camp cook in all the field trial world. Seasoned brown beans and corn dodgers were on the menu for the evening. Puddin cleaned his plate and was given seconds, as he thought the beans were about the best he had ever tried. He then made a makeshift bed on top of the lead truck. Saying a prayer just as he did every night at home, he quickly drifted off to sleep under the bright, twinkling stars above.

Arriving at Mr. Ike's North Dakota camp was an experience Puddin did not expect. The endless prairie grass was waving its golden hair over gently rolling, sculptured hills. This was in stark contrast to the endless, flat cotton fields and green Pine Hills of Mississippi. Puddin could not get over the lack of houses and people. It was like the whole of civilization had disappeared. There was nothing as far as the eye could see except for an old house, which would be the team's camp for the next two months.

Puddin helped take the anxious dogs out of the truck and into their new quarters for the summer. He then helped tote the camp supplies into the house where Spoon was already inspecting the wood cookstove, getting it ready to prepare a late supper for the camp. Repair work had started on the house, kennels, and stable, as Mr. Ike was itching to get the camp in order. A local rancher was bringing the horses the next morning. Mr. Ike had already firmly stated that he wanted to be ready to turn the first dogs loose by that late afternoon.

Sharing the bedroom with the two hands and Spoon, Puddin settled down on his bedroll spread on the worn wooden floor and wondered if he would live up to Mr. Moore's recommendation that he be brought along. He made a pact with himself that night to work hard, be respectful, keep his mouth shut and his ears open, and learn everything he could as fast as nature would allow. He wondered what his role would be in the operation and cautiously looked forward to learning about field trials and dogs.

The tantalizing aroma of home-cured bacon cooking in an iron skillet on a wood stove awoke Puddin well before sunrise. He quickly dressed and went into the kitchen, where the other hands and Mr. Ike were at the table drinking coffee and watching Spoon finish cooking eggs, bacon, grits, and biscuits and gravy. Mr. Ike spoke to Puddin. "Didn't know if you were going to join us this morning or not." During breakfast, each helper was given his instructions for the duration of their stay, including Puddin. "Clean out the kennels, feed and water the horses both morning and night, have the horses saddled and dog wagon horses hitched and ready to go at sunrise, and drive the dog wagon. You are also to help Spoon with the housecleaning and cooking."

The days on the prairie were long, but Puddin didn't mind. It was like stepping into a magical world with new sights and sounds all around him. While driving the dog wagon, he keenly watched everything Mr. Ike and the helpers did. How to style up dogs, road, and what a dog should look like pointing and running. He soaked up everything like a sponge. More and more Mr. Ike noticed Puddin observing the training process and knew through questions that Puddin was thinking about all he had seen. Ike was already considering changes in the camp assignments for the next summer, and Puddin was to be part of them.

The winter seemed to drag on forever, as Puddin had already been told he would be part of Mr. Ike's crew heading north the following summer. Over the winter, with the blessing of Mr. King, he was given the task of helping yard break puppies in the plantation's kennel. Given exact instructions by Mr. Ike in the manner he wanted the puppies started, Puddin followed his instructions to a T and was a natural with dogs. This did not go unnoticed by Ike and Mr. King. He also had the opportunity to attend trials that were held fairly close to the plantation. Riding next to Mr. King, he was responsible for his comfort and his horse. Mr. King was quick to explain to Puddin the ins and outs of trialing and the responsibilities of a scout. Puddin listened and hoped to be Mr. Ike's scout someday.

Finally the day came for Ike Moore's summer camp team to again make its way north for training and the prairie trials. The trucks were loaded, and it was time to depart. Puddin had just finished loading the last dog when he distinctly heard Mr. Ike say,

"Puddin, you are riding in my truck." Puddin froze, as he couldn't believe it. He knew it was true when Mr. Ike added, "You going with me or staying in Mississippi?" He quickly hopped in the Chevy, slammed the door, rolled down the window, and opened the vent. Off the crew went.

Puddin worked directly with Mr. Ike and the older dogs. A natural at horsemanship and with keen eyesight and a sixth sense when it came to getting into a dog's mind, Puddin had a shot at being a first-class dog trainer and scout. Mr. Ike added to Puddin's responsibilities as the long days of July became the first hot days of August.

Mr. King arrived at camp the first week of August with a good friend from Mississippi. He was to stay until the first prairie trials were finished, and his friend would stay for a week. Mr. King enjoyed his time with Puddin and was delighted to see his confidence in him had not been in vain. One day after kenneling and watering the dogs, Puddin witnessed Mr. Ike's longtime scout leaving the camp with the friend who had been camping for a week with the party. He could see Mr. King and Mr. Ike discussing something very important. Mr. King would scrape his boot on the dusty North Dakota soil, and Mr. Ike would take a long draw from his pipe as if in deep thought. After fifteen minutes, they made a beeline for Puddin. Mr. King spoke first. "Puddin, Ike and I have been discussing you and your future. Ike's scout has decided to go back home and quit field trialing. We both agree you are a natural with horses and dogs and would make a first-class scout. It's hard work but pays better. You would have to learn a great deal in a short period of time. What do you say?" Puddin stood in shock for a moment, then struggled out, "Yyyyyeeeeesssss, sir, I'll take the job and will try my best for you and Mr. Ike."

It was a whirlwind the next few weeks. Riding, watching, learning the tricks of the trade, and listening to Mr. Ike. Both the handler and the scout were in the beginning stages of a friendship that would last.

First came the August and September prairie trials. The first trial found Puddin as nervous as a pigeon darting from a hawk. When the brace was over, Mr. Ike rode up to Puddin and said that they were going to make a damn fine team and for him to just keep watching and learning. That he did, right up to the January trials leading to the National Championship. Mr. Ike said they were due for a win and due they were—a seven-find run had Puddin, with ten minutes left to go, spying his dog pointing, buried up in high grass and holding his head high. Now they had a win in a major trial qualifying them for Ames in February.

It was the most important day of his life, and Puddin was ready. The first brace of the fifth day of running at the National. Puddin and Mr. Ike had the big pointer in the best shape of his life. All they needed was a break or two and birds moving to feed. Never before had Puddin rode so hard. He was determined not to lose his dog in the maze of fields and woods that made up Ames. Nine perfect finds at the end of the day. Puddin had proved that he was an elite scout and as good as any. Mr. King said this was his proudest day. When the photos were taken on the steps of the manor house, both Ike and Mr. King insisted that Puddin kneel with the winning dog and be in the photograph with them.

In the years to come, Puddin and Mr. Ike traveled many miles together. Through rain, snow, hot, cold, dust—you name it—they were there together, a team that produced many other notable wins and another National Championship. Puddin took extra good care of Mr. Ike, as he was now in his late sixties and had slowed down just a bit.

It was a beautiful early June day with the sweet smell of honeysuckle heavy in the air when Puddin noticed a commotion at Mr. Ike's house, which was about a hundred yards from his. He ran to see if he could help, but it was too late. Mr. Ike lay dead in the front yard from a massive stroke. For the first time in his adult life, Puddin cried. The next day at the funeral he cried again. He was invited to sit with Ike's family, as they all said he was as much family as any of them.

A few days later, Mr. King came to see Puddin. They shared a cold Coke while sitting on the porch swing of the small house where he lived with his wife and two girls. Mr. King took a deep breath and said, "I guess you have been wondering what is going to happen now that we have lost Ike. I have studied on it a great deal and have decided to hire Jim Barnes as the new plantation boss and handler of my dogs in trials. I am going to step back a bit and enjoy life. I hope the two of you will get along fine. If you need me, I will be spending the summer at our house in Jackson."

Jim Barnes was known to be hard on his employees and dogs. Puddin couldn't explain how a fine man like Mr. King could hook up with such a worthless scoundrel such as Jim Barnes, but he decided to try hard to impress his new boss. What he didn't know was that his new boss had already hatched a plan to replace him as soon as they returned from the prairie trials. Not long after their arrival at Yancopin, Barnes came up to Puddin with a bottle in one hand and a bad attitude in the other. "You sorry SOB, we didn't win a thing on the prairies, and it's your fault. The dogs weren't ready, you didn't even give an effort to scout them, and I had some money missing and I know that hundred in your billfold is mine. You have one week to pack your belongings and get off this plantation." With that, he walked back to his house, sat down on the front porch swing, tipped his bottle towards Puddin, and had a drink.

Puddin was devastated; he had never known anything but Yancopin. He had met his wife there and raised his children within sight of the manor house. For the first time in his life he was afraid, as the future was not clear. He and his wife packed and loaded his old truck with no idea where they were going and what the future would hold.

A week passed, and Puddin stood by the truck, taking one last look at the place he loved. He opened the truck door, pressed down on the starter, and prepared to turn the key and get under way. His hand was turning the key when he heard a car horn sound. Looking up, he saw Mr. King's Cadillac. Slinging gravel and sliding to a stop, Mr. King exited the car quickly and said, “Wait just a New York minute. You’re not leaving yet.” Getting out of the truck, Puddin replied, “I got the keys to my house right here. I was going to leave them in the manor house mailbox. You will find the house is clean and is in better shape than when I moved in.”

Mr. King looked directly into Puddin’s eyes and said, “You better believe I want those keys. You’ll never need them again!” Then, reaching into his pocket, Mr. King produced another set of keys and handed them to Puddin. “These are the keys to the head trainer’s house Jim Barnes has been living in. I guess you have been too busy to notice that he’s been moving out. I don’t know where he’s going, but he will never set foot on this plantation again. You are the new head dog trainer of this plantation, and furthermore, I had written into my will that you and your wife may live in that house rent-free for the rest of your lives.” Puddin gave Mr. King a big hug and fondly thought that his good friend Mr. Ike must be looking down from heaven with a smile.

Three Cups of Coffee

The early rays of the bright orange Florida sunrise slowly inched their way in and touched the half-opened, bloodshot eyes of Leon Corbitt. An empty bottle of cheap Tennessee bourbon lay on the dusty, well-used night table by his bed. Closing his eyes, he thought why bother waking up at this early hour? It would just be a day wasted doing mundane tasks until another empty bottle, forced sleep and then awaking to an endless repetition of the same day. As Leon rolled over to shield himself from the approaching morning sun's uninvited touch, he became aware of the cause of his sleep's disruption.

"Hello in the house; is anyone home?" The shrill call through the open window seemed to bounce from wall to wall in endless echoes.

"Go away," Leon shouted, pulling a pillow over his head and hoping to again find peace in slumber.

"Hello in the house," the call came again, cutting the silence like a knife. "Mr. Charlie Henry told me you might want to lease your five hundred acres. I need a place loaded with birds to train my two bird dog pups."

Leon thought a moment. He needed the money. Rubbing his eyes, he replied, "The fee is steep: three hundred dollars."

The reply came crackling back. "I'll have hard cash in your hand by this afternoon."

It was October 1945. Leon had just returned to his family's farm in Florida after a tour of duty in the Pacific, specifically Okinawa. All he desired was to be left alone with his bottle and to forget the carnage and the friends he would never see again.

Leon was tall with thick black hair and dark brown eyes. He used to have a friendly smile, but that was long gone with the war. He was unkempt, with a week's worth of whiskers, and he was a fair amount of time away from a reunion with soap and a bathtub.

With the commotion of the morning, he reluctantly decided to get up, eat a two-egg breakfast, and tend the few cows left on the farm. Leon's parents had both passed away while he was serving in the Pacific. That left him the farm—and alone.

After tending the cattle and fixing a bit of fence, a sandwich was in order, along with a bourbon pick-me-up. As soon as he took the first bite of lunch, someone knocked on the door.

"Anyone inside?" came the same voice that woke him up that morning.

"Come in," Leon barked.

Lisa Brown and her sister Mary entered the house. Both young women were tall, with medium-length brown hair styled to the period. Dressed in jeans, they fit the bill for "farm girls."

"I've got your lease money here, along with an agreement I have written."

Leon signed it without looking, choosing to stare at the half-eaten sandwich rather than the girls.

"That's great," said Lisa with pleasure. "Here is the other six hundred."

"Six hundred!" exclaimed a shocked Leon, looking straight at Lisa. "The lease is for three hundred."

"Yes," Lisa said calmly. "The rest is your fee for helping us train the pups. The word is that, when sober, you are the best dog trainer in these parts. Mary and I are in agreement that we want the best training available for these special pups."

Leon angrily rose from the table and pointed a shaking finger at the women. "I ain't agreed to nothing of the kind. You can expect no help from me with your dogs. Now, take your six hundred dollars, find the door, and leave me alone!"

Lisa looked Leon straight in the eye and sternly replied, "This contract is for three hundred dollars lease and six hundred for four months of training services provided by a Mr. Leon Corbitt. You signed it. We will be back at sunrise tomorrow. Be ready!"

Leon was silent for a moment and then shouted, "You tricked me and I'll not honor the contract!"

As she left, Lisa nonchalantly replied, "You will find the six hundred on the table by the front door, sunrise tomorrow."

Leon poured a stiff drink and mumbled to himself, "I'll not work a day for those two, not one day."

The smell of bacon pried Leon's eyelids apart just a bit. Was this just another dream? He had a tough night between the bourbon and his nightmares of the war. As he slowly wiped the night's sleep from his eyes, he distinctly heard the clattering of pots from the kitchen and realized the aroma of bacon was real. Struggling to put on his twice-worn Levi's, he stumbled to the kitchen. There were Lisa and Mary, happily preparing eggs, bacon, and grits.

"What are you doing in my kitchen, and how did you get in here?" Leon demanded angrily.

"The front window was open," Mary replied as she placed once-over eggs on a plate. "It'll be sunrise in fifteen minutes. Sit down and eat your breakfast. We've got dogs to train."

"I'm not eating anything. Now, the both of you, get out," Leon, now red-faced, replied while pouring himself a morning libation. "This is all the breakfast I need."

"You can eat or not," came the answer. "Lisa and I prepared it, and we are going to enjoy it."

After breakfast, Lisa and Mary hurriedly cleaned up and headed outside. "You coming?" Lisa inquired as the screen door slapped shut.

"No," was the firm answer as Leon gave the screen door a push and then sat down on the porch swing, his drink in hand. The surroundings began to wake up to the new, warm October day.

"Where do you want to begin?" Lisa asked while unloading a beautiful white pointer male.

"Do what you want; I've got all I can handle in my hand on this porch." As Leon watched, the two sisters methodically took the pups through a beginning yard work drill that would have made any teacher proud.

After an hour of work, Mary loaded the pups into their truck while Lisa addressed Leon. "See you tomorrow. Leave the front door unlocked for breakfast."

The next two mornings, the exact scenario unfolded as Leon refused to help. On the third morning, he had an extra bourbon and was more agitated than normal at the presence of the women and their pups. When the training session ended, Leon staggered off the porch and loudly confronted the first of the two sisters he saw, which was Mary. At the top of his hateful voice, he shouted, "I'm tired of you and your sister poking your nose where it shouldn't be and trying to run my life. The two of you are nothing but trouble, and I demand to be left alone. You have no idea what I have been through and the things I have witnessed. You watched the war safe and comfortable in a movie theater while I lived out the newsreels. Take your sister, go home, and never show your face here again!"

Mary, frozen for a moment, broke into tears and ran to the truck, her sister not far behind. Lisa turned toward Leon before departing and gave him a stone-cold, fire-eyed look that he would never forget.

For the remainder of the day, he never left the front porch except to replace a dry glass or dusty bottle. That night, he lay awake thinking of his actions until the alcohol took effect and he began a night of unpleasant sleep and nightmares.

The next morning, he awoke to a pounding headache and the crowing of a rooster—not to the pleasant smell of bacon frying in an old iron skillet. Later in the day, he answered a knock at his door. It was Lisa, her dark eyes angry and fixed on his.

"In all my days, I never would have thought you would say such cruel and hurtful words to Mary. Training the pups and cooking breakfast for you were the first times she has left the house and really tried to get on with her life since her husband was killed in the last days of the war. Did you ever wonder why she didn't engage in conversation? Well, now you know! The training of the pups was to be her therapy, but now, through your drunken self-pity, she may never return to her old self. Sit, drink, and waste your pitiful life away. See if I care. I expect the quick return of the six hundred dollars training money." At this, Lisa turned and stomped away in tears.

Leon stood at the door a good long while, watching the dust settle as Lisa was quick to place distance between her truck and Leon's house. After the truck disappeared, he did as he had so many times before—poured himself a drink and drowned his memories.

A week to the day later, Mary opened the door of her neatly kept white wood frame home to Leon's knock. Lisa had come into the parlor with Mary. Yes, it was Leon, but his appearance had changed. His hair was combed and he was clean-shaven, with neatly ironed clothes and polished boots.

Clearing his throat, he began, "Miss Mary and Miss Lisa, I came to apologize for the shameful way I acted and treated you last week. There was no excuse. I would like to help train your pups if you will give me another chance. I'll be ready and sober tomorrow if you see fit to come." Neither Lisa nor Mary uttered a word as Leon turned and headed toward his old Ford truck.

That night, Leon did not drink but instead cleaned his home, which had been in rather rugged condition. He was up early, hoping against hope that the sisters would arrive before the morning sun. His heart jumped like a rabbit when he heard a truck door slam and footsteps on the porch. It was Lisa.

She came into the kitchen without a word and prepared breakfast. After eating, her first words were simply, "Let's get started. Mary is in the truck but will not get out. She still has not said a word since your actions toward her last week."

For the next two weeks, the pot of coffee was singing as Lisa arrived to cook breakfast for herself and Leon. She became more congenial to Leon as she gained confidence in the idea that he was sincere in his sobriety and truly wanted to help the sisters train the pups.

The first task for Leon and Lisa was to finish the yard breaking. The pups were of good breeding and never disappointed. Lisa was a quick learner and had all the makings of a first-class dog trainer. Days went by with the pups progressing nicely. Leon was proud of his accomplishments with the pups and his acceptance by Lisa. But he could not fully live a meaningful post-war life until Mary returned to normal and called him friend. She came to every one of the sessions but never left the passenger side of the truck.

After much thought to the words he would say, Leon decided it was time to talk to Mary. Lisa had stepped into the house, giving Leon the perfect moment to visit with her alone.

"Miss Mary, I have been wrong in so many ways. Both to you and your sister but also to myself. It would help me in my healing process if you would again eat breakfast in my house and help in the training of the pups. I give you my word of honor to be nothing but a gentleman." Mary did not say anything, but the tears streaming down her cheeks told of emotions that had been held inside for too long. Leon kindly thanked her for her time, turned, and loaded the dogs into the wooden dog box in the truck and walked away.

Monday came early for Leon as he nervously awaited the arrival of the sisters. The coffee was hot, and three cups were placed on the table in hopeful anticipation. The screen door opened with a squeak, as it had so many times before, but this time there was the glorious sound of two pairs of footsteps. Leon was both relieved and anxious. Lisa and Leon exchanged pleasantries, but Mary did not speak.

After breakfast, the three began the last few days of yard work before the pups would be turned loose to run in front of horses, beginning their preparations for field trials. Mary helped and followed Leon's suggestions to a T but did not speak except to Lisa and the pups.

During these last few days of yard work, Lisa noticed Leon paying particular attention to Mary and Mary becoming more comfortable with him. On Friday afternoon, Leon told the sisters that Monday would involve the pups running in the field with them mounted on horses and they should come prepared to ride.

Upon arriving bright and early Monday morning at Leon's home, Lisa and Mary noticed three horses tied to a fence, saddled and ready to go. Breakfast was quickly prepared and eaten in anticipation of the exciting events to come. Leon first helped Lisa get up on her horse and then Mary. Leon was shocked when Mary looked down at him and said in a kind and gentle voice, "Thank you very much."

After these few words, the world seemed a bit brighter and happier to Leon, as this was the first time he had ever heard Mary speak. The morning was full of trials, experimentation, errors, fun, and frustration. Both pups showed potential and seemed to be natural frontrunners. The sisters were getting a crash course in how to be not only trainers but also handlers.

For two months, not only did the pups become more proficient but the sisters proved to be fast learners as well. Eventually, Leon and Mary became friends and then good friends. This met with Lisa's approval, as Mary's old self was showing more and more each day.

One winter morning close to Christmas, Leon sat eating breakfast with the two and said, "Would you consider six more months with me at the same salary?"

Lisa and Mary looked at each other and smiled. They both let out a big, "Yes!"

Leon cracked a smile and then took on a serious tone. "We have worked the pups hard, and now it's time to show them off to the world. I really think you've got something in those two. The South Central Derby Classic will be held close by in a month. Let's enter both dogs."

The sisters clapped their hands in approval. "Wait a minute," Leon continued. "I am going to scout the pups, so you will have to be the handler."

This took the smile off the sisters' faces and gave them reason to pause. After thinking, Lisa slowly said, "Let's get the dogs ready." Mary nodded her head in agreement. Lisa decided to handle their hardheaded male and Mary the petite female. Serious questions were asked, with dog work following as the threesome geared up for the Classic.

The big day finally arrived with all three being both excited and extremely nervous. The first to run was Lisa's big male. One find and a back. Not bad at all for the first time, Leon thought.

Mary and her little female were scheduled to run two braces later. When the dust cleared, Mary's charge had three finds coupled with a beautiful forward race. She had just handled her first winner.

The next evening, Leon was driving by the sisters' house and noticed Mary sitting on the porch swing. He pulled in the driveway, got out, and slowly climbed the porch steps. "I've wanted to share a few things with you for a long time. Maybe this is as good a time as any. I am truly glad you are doing so much better, and I'm thankful I had a small part in it. You and Lisa saved me from a life of pity and the bottle. What you see of me today is in a large part due to you and Lisa. I am forever in your debt." He was a bit embarrassed and turned to leave.

Mary stopped him and gave him the biggest hug of his life. "You helped save me," Mary said while wiping away a tear. "I am better today due to your friendship and understanding."

This bonded a lifelong friendship between Lisa, Mary, and Leon that lasted fifty wonderful years until his death in 1997. Both Lisa and Mary went on to marry and raise families. Leon became one of the most successful field trialers in history. He campaigned many great dogs, including a steady stream of pointers from the sisters. Leon never married, but he enjoyed a full life, living just down the road from Lisa and Mary, who helped introduce him to the good things life has to offer. Until their deaths, the sisters would meet at Leon's grave on his birthday and carry three coffee cups and a thermos of hot coffee in honor of their friend whom they dearly loved like a brother.

The Bond

It was a cold December day in 1940 when Bill Prior and Don Henry met on a fence row between two cotton fields in the Arkansas delta. Bill had a pointer who had been loosed on the south end while Don had turned loose his setter on the north end. The dogs were located on point almost simultaneously by their youthful handlers.

"My dog's got the point," said Bill.

"You don't know anything. My dog was here first," demanded Don.

What started out as a fun Saturday afternoon turned into a few punches being thrown and rolling around on the ground until their youthful exuberance flushed the covey. The wrestling match ended as the covey took flight and disappeared without a shot being fired.

Bill looked at his counterpart and asked, "Where did you come from? I've never seen you before."

Don replied, "We just moved here from Mississippi. My dad's foreman on the number nineteen canal project. Hey, is your pointer any good?"

"As good as any setter, I reckon," Bill replied in a lower tone. "Let's turn 'em loose and see."

From that not-so-auspicious beginning, the two boys were inseparable. During bird season, they could be found hunting during any spare time. On hot summer days, they fished for bream in Cypress Creek.

During high school, Bill and Don played basketball, ran track, and always double-dated together. At the end of their senior year, they entered the same college with, of course, the same major. Both met their soulmate in college and were the other's best man. Settling down after college to a successful business, each had two children, a boy and a girl.

After their families, bird hunting and running dogs was their passion. The only differentiation between the two, that friends and family could see, was Don's passion for setters and Bill's for pointers. Many a winter day was spent in the field with one or the other bragging of the superior traits of their breed of dog. Bill would brag that his pointer could cover twice the ground as Don's setters while Don fired back that his setter could find twice the birds. These friendly barbs would go back and forth between the two whether in the field, at home, or in the coffee shop.

Throughout the years, where Don was, Bill was sure to follow and vice versa. The friends were there for each other during the sickness and death of parents, as well as the joy connected with the birth and weddings of their children.

As retirement neared, Bill asked Don one day, "Have you ever thought of retiring to Florida where the winters are a bit kinder to old folk's bones?" Bill replied, "It's strange that you would bring this up, as my wife and I discussed the same subject last night." So it came to pass that both friends ended up in southwest Florida, living as next door neighbors. They found the Florida winters kind to their constitution as well as providing a new game to play, field trialing. Training together, they learned the intricacies of field trialing and finding birds in south Florida. They trained every opportunity possible from September to March, becoming even closer friends as father time progressed.

Don would never forget the date, October 7, 2014. They had dogs draped over the saddle and were heading home in the late twilight of a comfortable Florida evening after a few hours of training. Bill said, "Don, I've got something to tell you. As you know, I went to see my doctor yesterday, and he informed me that tests confirmed an aggressive, untreatable cancer. He gave me no more than two months to live. I want to spend as much time with you and my family as possible in the days I have remaining."

Don, not knowing quite what to say, nodded his head and after a few minutes silence, said, "You are like family to me. We will run dogs and trial as long as you are able." Pausing another long minute, he continued, "Besides, you have yet to prove the advantage of a pointer over a setter!" The men looked at each other and smiled. The remainder of ride was spent with each man silently recalling the good times with their best friend.

In late November, returning from a short training session, Bill turned toward Don and thoughtfully said, "I think this will have to be my last trip running dogs. I can feel my time is growing very short. Will you take care of my wife and dogs after I am gone?"

Don said, "Of course, my friend."

Bill then said, while admiring the beautiful Florida sunset through the scattered pines for the last time, "Even after my passing, I promise to always be with you when you ride and train in this special place." No more needed to be said as both friends enjoyed the beauty of the early evening and their last run together.

Two weeks later, Bill's ashes were scattered at the field trial grounds he loved with his loving family and friends present. Bill had picked a favorite place for his final resting place. Stories were told with both laughter and tears and good-byes said.

Don's field trial club had their largest and most prestigious trial scheduled for the New Year's holiday. Bill and Don had sculpted some of their most special memories at this trial. After Bill's death, Don told his wife that he just didn't have the heart to participate this year. However, at the urging of his wife, he decided to take his pointer and Bill's setter out for a run just before Christmas to see how the dogs would do, and more importantly, to see if he had the heart to run without his dear friend.

The late afternoon was typical southwest Florida December weather as Don headed the dogs back to camp to conclude his training session. Just a bit of a chill from a northwest breeze tickling the palmettoes to both sides, a beautiful blue sky, and a sunset so stunning, surely an artist had painted the masterpiece. Don could not help thinking of Bill as they had enjoyed many evenings such as this. There was no question things were just not the same as before. Time had taken a part of his soul which could not be filled again. He recalled the promise of his friend and wished it could truly be so. The memories of a lifetime passed before him as well as the beauty of the day. He knew he would not return as things were just not fun. Life, unfortunately, would never be the same.

Suddenly, nearing the area where Bill's ashes were scattered, a strange feeling of happiness and wellbeing filled him. Giving a deep sigh, and adjusting himself in the saddle, he looked for the dogs and there it was. Don stopped his horse, rubbed his eyes and stared in utter disbelief. The image was very plain; there was absolutely no mistake. Bill's shadow was cast upon the ground not far from his. Don had seen this same shadow hundreds of times while training with Bill. The promise had been kept and the friendship renewed.

Don continued to train and trial, making a point to always look for Bill's shadow, which would often accompany him when working dogs. Upon Don's death, both families agreed that the friends would continue running dogs in eternity, as there are some special bonds that even death cannot part.

Image courtesy of Petie Brown

The Wolves of Crow Mountain

Perhaps, back in the 1950s, the premier all-age trial grounds between Florida and the prairies was the Arkansas Classic, whose courses meandered around Crow Mountain in northwest Arkansas. The open fields and tree-lined edges were prime habitat for quail. It was not uncommon for braces to produce five or six coveys.

All the major handlers brought their A game to this most prestigious trial, including the best dogs and scouts the sport has ever known. Heading up the field was George Harrell, his scout, Bill “Big” King, and Don Cruse and his equally illustrious scout, Mike “Slick” Oates. These two handlers and scouts were fierce competitors and were not exactly enemies—but certainly not church pew–sitting friends. Most years, George and Don would be neck and neck for handler of the year, but for some reason, George could never beat Don at the Classic. A fact that stuck in George’s throat like a chicken bone.

Whenever Don needed another find to win, invariably his dog would produce one in a small holler by the mountain. The holler was protected by a thin stand of trees and was a perfect habitat for quail inside. It seemed that Don was the only handler whose dogs could find birds in this area.

Over the years, it was a well-known fact within scout circles that this holler was haunted and contained vicious wolves. Rumors also circulated that a lone rider, attempting to enter the holler, would be met by a howling, evil spirit and subsequently be attacked by wolves. Several scouts, including Big, had attempted to follow their dogs into the holler only to be met by the hair-raising howl of the evil spirit. Any who had tried and heard the howl would never try again. Only one scout had ever seen the inside of this holler: Don's scout, Slick.

When asked by the other scouts how he could enter the holler, he told this story. "I comes from south Louisiana. They's a voodoo queen there who knows different spells and magic charms which keeps evil spirits away. I have one around my neck right now. The evil spirits and wolves ain't gonna harm me."

Don and George drew the last brace of the trial. Both handlers and their scouts planned to ride all the braces to get reacquainted with the course. After fifteen minutes into the first brace, Big noticed Slick starting to get farther and farther behind the gallery until he was out of sight of all except Big, who had hung back and followed him, careful to not reveal himself. The farther Slick went, the more confident Big became that he was heading for the wolf holler.

When Slick reached the line of trees before the entrance, a man popped out from behind a tree. He reached out and accepted what looked like money. The man then quickly disappeared into the tree line.

This looked highly suspicious to Big. He stayed hidden for a few minutes and then mounted and headed directly through the trees to the holler. All of a sudden, he heard a frightening howl. This time he was not scared, as the howl came from the same area the man had disappeared into. Big turned his horse and quickly rode away from the holler just as he and other scouts had done many time before. He was not running away but rather formulating a plan of action.

That night, Big visited a good friend who lived about a mile from the trial grounds. This friend and his two German shepherds were about to become an integral part of Big's plan, which would change the fortunes of many present and future handlers of the Arkansas Classic.

Arriving back at the scout quarters, he made his way to Slick. "Slick, I was talking to some of the boys. They got too close to the wolf holler when riding back to the clubhouse after the last brace of the day. They heard the spirit howl and swore they caught a glimpse of a wolf stalking 'em. I'm not going in that holler, ever." The seed had been cleverly planted.

Before sunrise the next morning, Big told George his stomach was a bit upset. He assured him he would be able to ride for their brace in the afternoon, but he might miss being a spectator and riding the first brace of the day. Big then slipped out of camp and headed toward the wolf holler. Just before the tree line, he met up with his friend who had his two German shepherds with him. Big questioned, "Now, you is sure these two dogs ain't goin' to hurt anybody, is they? Just scare 'em?"

The friend confidently answered him. "All they is goin' to do is grab this man's pants legs and scare the ever-lovin' daylight out of him."

Sure enough, right after daylight, here came the mystery man, followed shortly by Slick. As soon as Slick handed off the regular payment, Big let out two howls that even the most ardent unbeliever would have sworn came from an underworld spirit. Right after the howls, the shepherds were released and grabbed the legs of the man's overalls while growling ferociously.

The man screamed and started to run the best he could with the shepherds nipping at his heels. Slick, in the meantime, had his horse at a full run and was last seen putting as much distance between himself and what he thought were attacking wolves.

Big paid his friend three dollars for the use of his dogs and rode back to camp.

That afternoon, George won the Classic for the first time. Big rode into the holler and found their dog pointing while Slick did everything in his power to turn his dog away from the haunted holler and its wolves! From that year forward, George and his scout Big won their share of Arkansas Classic championships, many of them won pointing the wolf holler covey. And for some reason, Don and Slick never won the Classic again.

Heaven

Junior Smith, Roger Blevins, and Jimmy Lee were in their middle teens when they first skipped school to be in the gallery of the old Southwestern trial held on the sanatorium grounds near Booneville, Arkansas. They clearly remembered Marshall Loftin, Hoyle Eaton, John Rex Gates, Man Rand, and many of the other personalities, handlers, scouts, and dogs connected to the trial.

All three had taken up field trialing as amateurs and had been very successful. Many years later, they met for afternoon coffee on a cold, crisp November afternoon in Booneville, where all three made their home. The conversation turned to their memories of the Southwestern trial, as this week was the traditional starting date. After laughs about skipping school and discussion regarding famous dogs and scouts, the trio decided to make a quick trip to the grounds to see if the old clubhouse was still standing and shaking its fist at time.

Arriving just before dusk, the men exited Jimmy's truck and stared at the clubhouse, which was, remarkably, still standing. Junior broke the silence and said, "I still remember Robert Burris at the foot of Hen Scratch Mountain with a distant view of White

Knight. My favorite dog was Monte Bello Peggy; she looked like a statue on point."

All of a sudden, the conversation was cut short by a cold, wet breeze that almost took the visitors' breath away. Simultaneously, a fog appeared out of nowhere, rising from the ground as if in a Hollywood movie. Turning in tandem, the trio started back to the truck, all sensing it was time to go.

Junior turned for one last look and grabbed Roger's arm with a firm grip. "Did you see that?"

"What?" Roger replied, expecting a bobcat or deer.

"I saw a light in the clubhouse."

"You saw what?" Roger looked straight at the weathered building in the near darkness.

"I'm not crazy. I know what I saw, and I saw a light in that building."

Just as Jimmy turned to look, all three saw it. A dim, orange-yellow light and what looked like a figure moving between it and the window.

Jimmy spoke up. "Who's in there?"

No answer came, but the light disappeared in sync with Jimmy's first word. Puzzled, the men drove off asking the same question, "Who was in the clubhouse and for what reason?" A decision was quickly made to come back the next afternoon and do some detective work.

The next afternoon, the old gathering place appeared remarkably well preserved for its age and lack of care. The roof leaked and windowpanes were broken, but it was otherwise intact. Upon investigation, other than a few critters and a bird or two, the inside showed absolutely no signs of use. Their questions of the previous evening were only answered by more questions that afternoon. As they were no nearer to solving the mystery than before the investigation, the decision was made to wait outside in the same place as the night before.

Exactly as the previous night, the same light appeared, accompanied by the cold, moist breeze and the fog. This time there looked like several figures casting shadows between the light and the window. The men remained silent in anticipation of what might happen next. Then, faint sounds of horses and whispers could be heard, the sound carried by the cold wind. By this time the men were shivering, as the temperature had dropped significantly from the time of their arrival.

Junior saw them first, then the other two men: a woman and two men on horseback, coming out of the heart of the fog, headed toward the clubhouse.

Adjusting his weight, Roger stepped on a twig and snapped it. The sound was not loud but enough to be heard in the early twilight. The three figures looked directly at the source of the sound revealing the trespassers and then disappeared into the night.

Heading back to Booneville, there was no discussion—just silence. The trio was doing their best to digest what they had just witnessed. Arriving in Junior's driveway, Roger spoke. "What in the world did we just see?"

There was silence for a minute, then Jimmy slowly and thoughtfully said, "All I know is that there were three horses and three riders. We all witnessed that. After those facts, it's anyone's guess. What I cannot grasp is how they looked at us before they disappeared. I don't know what we have stepped into, but one thing is for sure: I want to go back."

The trio was in agreement; they would go back the next night.

Arriving the following night, the three witnessed the light in the clubhouse only to see what looked like more activity inside. The smell of burning wood and smoke exiting the fireplace was witnessed along with the faint, sweet smell of supper being prepared. Disbelief showed on the face of each man. All of a sudden, the temperature plummeted as the frigid fog rolled in quickly, accompanied by muffled voices and the sound of horses.

Unlike the night before, there were several horses and riders. There were also some dogs attached to the saddles by ropes. Upon arriving, the group unsaddled the horses and headed into the clubhouse. Before entering, the three figures that had been witnessed last night turned and looked directly at the white-faced onlookers. Their facial features were prominent and could clearly be seen, although there was a ghostly appearance to them. They looked at the men for what seemed like a lifetime and then turned and went in to join the gathering.

Just then, another rider of African-American descent appeared out of the fog with an all-white dog draped across the saddle. The man looked at the three, nodded his head, gave the dog a pat, and disappeared into the fog.

The trio stayed longer, but no other activity occurred except in the clubhouse. Unlike the first night, the light did not disappear.

Turning onto the highway, Jimmy slapped the steering wheel and said, "I got a good look at some of the men, the lady, and the last rider. You're going to think I'm crazy, but they look familiar."

Roger and Junior chimed in and said the same thing. Each man had his own ideas about the faces they had seen but kept those impressions to themselves.

"I've got a thought," Junior said. "My granddaughter is an art instructor at Booneville High School and is very talented. Let's see if she can create a sketch of the woman from our description."

The meeting was arranged and the session started. When the sketch was completed, the three stared at each other. The color had left their faces. "This is not possible," Junior slowly said, looking directly at Roger and Jimmy.

Roger stared wide-eyed at the sketch and then cautiously replied, "It can't be, but it is."

Jimmy whispered, "It's been so long; we were in our teens."

"We've got to be sure," Roger said, giving another look at the lady. "Let's take this sketch and show it to old Mr. Shillings. He judged the Southwestern more years than we can count."

All were in agreement that this was an excellent idea. On the way, there was ample conversation in the truck but not a word uttered regarding what they knew was almost certain fact.

Walking up the white sidewalk to Mr. Shillings's front door, Jimmy tightly gripped the folder that contained the sketch, as if it might somehow disappear into the winter wind. They were greeted at the door by a man who had seen most of the great dogs and handlers since the early 1950s.

"We have something to show you," Roger said, handing the folder to Mr. Shillings, who was putting on a pair of reading glasses.

He looked at the sketch, removed his glasses, and gave a puzzled look to the three gentlemen. "Why, that's Mary Oliver. No mistake about it. For some reason, I was just thinking about her the other day. Where did you get this?"

"Mr. Shillings, that sketch was done today from descriptions we gave." Jimmy said. He paused and gave a long exhale. "You may think we are crazy, but . . . the three of us just saw her last night riding up to the old Southwestern clubhouse." They then recounted the whole unbelievable story, not leaving out one detail.

After the story was finished, Mr. Shillings did not bat an eye but rather pointed a shaking finger right at them and, with sparkling eyes, said, "Let me tell you a tale. As it became obvious that we would not be able to keep the Southwestern going at Booneville, the whole lot of us were in the clubhouse one afternoon because of a weather delay. We began to talk and reminisce along with a glass or two of pick-me-up. It was agreed on that rainy day, and sealed with a toast, that if possible, after our time on earth was through, to meet at the clubhouse once a year, enjoy old times, and have another trial. Yes sir, it looks like some have found their way to again run a dog with the best there ever was and ever will be!

"I want to go with you tonight. I know I'll slow you down, but I've just got to go," Mr. Shillings implored.

The trio unanimously agreed, and in the late afternoon, the quartet set out for another adventure.

Just like the previous nights, with the last rays of the sun tickling the winter landscape, a light came on in the clubhouse. There were unrecognizable figures moving about and the unmistakable aroma of supper being prepared. The cold, damp fog appeared just as before, but this time there were many ghostly riders, slowly appearing out of the fog, heading toward the clubhouse.

"I can't believe my eyes," Mr. Shillings softly murmured. "That's Mary Oliver and Leon Covington. And look, that's . . . that's . . . Robert Burris with White Knight over his saddle. I know them all. It's all my friends. They're here, they're really here."

The figures dismounted and headed into the clubhouse. Before entering through the door, they turned and looked straight at the mesmerized men. The look was only for a few seconds but seemed like an eternity for the quartet. It was as if the figures were looking for something or someone.

Silently, the men made their way back to the truck. After the motor was started, Mr. Shillings broke the heavy silence and in a hushed tone said, "It was like they were looking squarely at me, trying to tell me something. This is just incredible. Thank you for taking me to see this." Upon exiting the truck after it arrived at his home, Mr. Shillings again thanked the trio, paused, then took a slow walk to his front door.

Early the next morning, Jimmy's phone rang. It was Junior. "I just got the sad word that Mr. Shillings passed away peacefully in his sleep last night."

That afternoon, Jimmy, Junior, and Roger paid their respects to Mr. Shillings's family. Upon leaving the house, the sun was heavy and starting to set.

"I want to go back to the old clubhouse," Junior said, his eyes fixed on the winter horizon as if he were looking for answers to questions that have no answer. The other two men agreed as their eyes also searched the horizon for clues.

When they arrived at the clubhouse, the light of the full moon was competing with the setting sun. As before, a chill came over the men, but this time it was different. This chill was not like any other they had experienced in their lives—it was cold, damp, and penetrating. Then came the arrival of the fog and the sound of riders and horses, which seemed to appear within the bat of an eye. There were many more riders than before. There they were: John

S. Gates, Stub Poynor, Peck Kelley, Man Rand, Mary Oliver, Leon Covington, and more. The men stood transfixed, as if time had opened up for this moment and the night was rolling back to the golden era of field trials. As the group headed into the clubhouse, one figure stopped, turned, and looked deep into the eyes of the three men. This look was longer than any look before, one that seemed to penetrate their very souls. Slowly turning, the figure waved at the men and proceeded into the clubhouse.

Junior finally said it as they headed back to the truck. "That was Mr. Shillings."

The other two shook their heads in disbelief and agreement.

All three made a pact on the way home to never mention the events of the past evenings to anyone and to never return to the old clubhouse in their mortal life. They did agree to meet at the clubhouse with all the other shades, after their passing, to once again experience the running of the Southwestern.

What is heaven? If a hundred people were asked, there would likely be a hundred answers. A good friend of mine who only had weeks to live conveyed this to me: She said, "How can heaven be heaven without the people we love and the things we love to do? When we meet again, I'll be at my favorite grounds running my favorite dog. We'll pick up our friendship like we have never been apart."

So who is to say that in November, on the week when the old Southwestern was contested, there is not a gathering of eternal friends again feeling the cold wind in their face, following the dogs they love so dearly.

Even in this technologically advanced world, there are still many occurrences that cannot be explained. Could this really happen? Possibly. The only way to find out for sure would be to travel to the Southwestern grounds on a November evening and find out for yourself.

The Christmas Present

Seven-year-old Sam Evans lived with his mother Liz and his father Bobby in a cozy, white frame house on the Rankin plantation in Rankinville, Florida. Bobby was the head dog trainer and handler of the plantation's string of field trial dogs. Plantation owner Henry Rankin and his wife Betty considered Bobby and Liz their children, as they had no children of their own. When not at school, Sam used the plantation as his personal playground and knew the entire acreage like the back of his hand. His happiest days were filled with riding with Bobby, chasing bird dogs, and learning the secrets of training. Since the time Sam could venture out of the house on his own, he and Bobby were inseparable.

Perhaps the finest dog to ever be bred on the plantation grounds was 1950 National Champion Rankin's Rebel Yell, call name Reb. Reb won the championship going away at age seven but suffered a back injury, which ended his field trial career. Reb was given to Sam by Mr. Rankin as a pet and was used as a stud dog, although sparingly. Next to his mom and dad, Reb was the love of Sam's life. He slept with Sam, and he had his place on the floor by the dinner table to collect any scraps that happened to come his way. Always first to greet Sam when he got off the school bus, Reb was truly Sam's dog.

Although not able to perform as a field trial dog, Reb had plenty of energy to keep up with Sam and his exploits around the plantation. If Sam was around the house, Reb was with him. Whether Sam was playing football or baseball, Reb was there. The only activity Reb was not allowed to do was go on workouts when Bobby worked dogs with Sam tagging along. They were considered dangerous because of his injury. There was no doubt that Reb still had the fire in his eye and desire in his heart to bound again among the pine-dotted stretches of the plantation, searching for the bobwhite for which he was bred to find.

Mid-December of 1954 found the plantation and town of Rankinville buzzing with excitement as the running of the Pine Tree Classic was about to begin. The best dogs and handlers in the world would be in town, including guests who would be riding many of the braces. Not a hotel room was available within miles of the town. Breakfast at the local restaurant was almost reservations only as everyone wanted in on the morning trial news and gossip more than the biscuits, gravy, and grits being served.

Bobby was running in the last brace, with Mr. Rankin riding in the gallery beside Sam in the early afternoon. It was sunny with a light, warm wind as the dogs were turned loose. Everyone viewing the brace expected a thrilling contest between two superior dogs. Five minutes after the breakaway, most in the gallery, including Bobby and the two judges, noticed a streak of white dart past the gallery and to the front. Bobby took a second look and said, "Reb!" Yes, there went eleven-year-old Reb darting to the front like a derby hot for game. Bobby, with the permission of the judges, sent Sam, who was riding in the gallery, after Reb. Bobby began to worry near the end of his brace, as there was no sign of Sam or Reb. As soon as the brace concluded, Bobby set out looking for the missing child and dog. After some time and much concern, he spotted Sam, still in a hunt for Reb, just as the last pale orange tone of the sunset sank behind the outline of the pine-filled horizon.

"Dad, I can't find him anywhere. I saw him for a moment about two hours ago far to the front. I'm worried. We've just got to find Rebel!"

Bobby consoled Sam and told him, "Reb knows this plantation. He'll make it home."

Bobby and Sam headed home just after dark without Reb. They grabbed a quick bite of a bologna sandwich that Liz had quickly made.

"Bobby, you've just got to find Reb. That dog means everything to Sam," Liz said, glancing down the plantation road at a truck now turning into their driveway.

Mr. Rankin and Betty quickly got out of the Chevy truck, and Mr. Rankin asked, "Have you found Reb?"

"No," was the reply from Bobby. "We are going out again to look in another area in case Reb missed the bend in the course."

"I'll help," replied Mr. Rankin. The search went on till almost midnight with no result. Sam was beside himself with worry and could not sleep without his friend beside him in bed.

The search for Reb was nonstop the next day. Bobby allowed Sam to miss school to help look for Reb. Mr. Rankin brought three of the plantation employees to help with the search. As darkness overtook the searchers, they rode back to Bobby's house with their heads down. Sam had been brave until this time, but the disappearance of his friend coupled with exhaustion drove him to tears. "Mr. Rankin, we're not going to find Reb—I just know it."

Mr. Rankin replied, "Let's give it another day. I'll have every plantation worker out looking for him." He gave Sam a loving pat on the back as they headed for home.

Sam climbed on the school bus the next day knowing that he would not have his mind on schoolwork. He hoped against hope that Reb would be found alive and unharmed.

Mr. Rankin directed his workers in what areas to search. "You go out and don't you come back until that dog is found." Not long after leaving Bobby's house, a shout was heard. "Over here, I've found him!" A mad dash was made by all to the vicinity of the call.

There, close to an abandoned house, lay the lifeless Reb. The search crew was silent for quite a while and then Bobby spoke. "Reb always had the heart of a lion. He wanted desperately to have one last run; I could see it in his eyes every day when we would leave to work dogs without him. He got that run. There usually is a covey in this area, and I like to think he died on point doing what he loved."

Rebel was taken to Bobby's house to await Sam. Mr. Rankin and Betty waited along with Bobby and Liz for Sam to make his way off the school bus and onto the front porch. "Did you find Reb?" Sam asked while looking in the yard for him.

Bobby replied, "Yes, Sam, we did, but the strain of the running was too much for him. We found him by the old home place laying in some brown grass, dead." Bobby struggled to hold back tears but could not. He had lost his best friend in the world. Equally feeling the pain, Mr. Rankin and Betty shed tears along with Bobby and Liz.

After a bit, Reb was buried. In the few heartfelt words that were said over the grave were mentions of the 1950 National Championship, his love for Sam, and that he died doing what he loved.

Christmas was only a few days away, which made Reb's passing difficult for Sam and his mom and dad. It seemed like there was no joy in the season, as everywhere the family looked, they expected to see Reb as he had become an iatrical part of the life of the Evans family.

Christmas morning began as the family opened presents, but they did not have the normal joy associated with the occasion. Sam was still mourning the passing of his friend with a heavy heart. After Christmas dinner, there was a familiar knock on the front door, recognizable as Mr. Rankin's. Through the door came Mr. Rankin and Betty with smiles on their faces.

"Merry Christmas!" Mr. Rankin exclaimed while setting a box on the floor. "Sam, take a look in the box. It's your Christmas present." Sam looked in, and looking back at him was a male black and white pointer pup. "Go ahead and take him out. He's yours, but I want you to know this is no ordinary puppy. He is out of the last litter Reb sired, and Betty and I want you to have him."

Sam's eyes sparkled as he gently picked up the pup and lovingly placed him in his lap. The bond between boy and dog took no longer than that. Sam now had a part of Reb to carry on the friendship. That night, with the pup curled up next to him in bed, Sam thought of his friend Reb and gave thanks for the new pup entrusted to him. In the following years, the pup lived a long life and often reminded Sam of Reb and the best Christmas present of his life.

About the Author

Robert Franks has been involved with bird dogs since being introduced to bird hunting in 1981. Field trialing has been part of his life since 1998. He retired after thirty-five years in education, with twenty-eight of those years spent as principal of DeWitt Elementary School in DeWitt, Arkansas.

www.ingramcontent.com/pod-product-compliance
Lightning Source LLC
Chambersburg PA
CBHW030815310726
48980CB00006B/501/J
* 9 7 8 0 5 7 8 3 1 8 0 1 1 *